P9-DNL-089

ADAM
CANFIELD
WATCH YOUR BACK!

ADAM
CANFIELD
WATCH YOUR BACK!

MICHAEL WINERIP

CANDLEWICK PRESS
CAMBRIDGE, MASSACHUSETTS

Copyright © 2007 by Michael Winerip

First edition 2007

Library of Congress Cataloging-in-Publication Data

Winerip, Michael, date.
Adam Canfield, watch your back! / Michael Winerip. —1st ed.
p.   cm.
Summary: A much-welcomed snow day turns into an embarrassing nightmare for
middle-grader Adam Canfield when, after being mugged by high-school bullies for
his snow-shoveling money, he becomes the focus of major media attention just as
fellow reporters at *The Slash* are launching a contest to out bullies at their school.
ISBN 978-0-7636-2341-8
[1. Bullying—Fiction. 2. Newspapers—Fiction. 3. Journalists—Fiction.
4. Middle schools—Fiction. 5. Schools—Fiction.]   I. Title.
PZ7.W72494Ade 2007
[Fic]—dc22   2007025245

2 4 6 8 10 9 7 5 3 1

Printed in the United States of America

This book was typeset in Slimbach.

Candlewick Press
2067 Massachusetts Avenue
Cambridge, Massachusetts 02140

visit us at www.candlewick.com

For my brother, Steve

chapter 1
Shovels of Troubles

Adam had never opened up such a big lead. When he glanced over his shoulder at the other runners, they were so far back, he had to admit that he almost felt sorry for their sad, little turtle legs. But still he picked up his pace to make a point. Glancing that way again, he saw that they were gone. Victory was sweet; total victory, totally sweet. But wait. If this was total victory, what was that uneasy feeling creeping over him? Was he really that far in front? Or had he taken a wrong turn and gotten lost again? Please, anything but that. As he reviewed the race in his mind, he realized that it wasn't so much a question of being lost, as—wasn't there something he had to do? He definitely had a nagging, squirmy feeling, then worse, an unmistakable ache, a sense that there was very urgent business to attend to.

Pee! He had to pee! He opened his eyes. The bedroom was dark. Of course it was. Those six glasses of water before bed—the Adam Canfield 100 percent foolproof wake-up system. It had worked! He raced to the window. Snow! Beautiful snow, lots of it. The street, the bushes, the sidewalks, and cars were all covered in a thick coat of frosty, white, unspoiled snow, and it was still coming down heavily. No way there'd be school on Friday. Adam was beaming. And chilled. He rushed to the bathroom, rushed back to bed, buried himself under the covers, thrust both hands into his boxers, and curled into a ball. Lying there, he tried to get himself back to that lead in the running club race.

But in the morning, there were no new dreams to remember.

/////

Adam shoveled his own walk and driveway quickly, then went looking for jobs. He was in high spirits. The snow was good for shoveling: wet enough so it didn't blow off the shovel but not too wet — it wouldn't just melt away. Usually, the Tri-River Region got only two or three big storms a winter, so Adam wanted to get as many jobs as possible. On his best day of shoveling ever, he had made two hundred dollars.

First up was the house across the street. They wanted Adam to shovel whenever it snowed. He didn't even have to ring the bell, and later they'd leave the thirty dollars in his mailbox. Older people like them didn't want to do anything to aggravate their clogged arteries, so they were happy to pay. Some other customers were weird, though. The next woman stood outside watching Adam the whole time. She wanted only half her driveway cleared — said she had just one car. And she wanted her walk done just one shovel wide. She supervised every shovelful, as if Adam were going to steal her snow. He finished fast, but all she paid was ten dollars.

He walked down the center of the street, between the high banks that the snowplows had made, to where the block dead-ended at the Tremble River, then headed along the back path. To get a look at the river, he climbed a bluff, barreling upward through the undisturbed snow. He loved stepping in unstepped-in snow and then tumbling back down.

He brushed off, then placed the shovel over his shoulder and marched up the next street. It was getting colder and windier. The wet snow would soon ice over, making the shoveling harder. Adam might be forced to charge double.

He did a big house that took almost an hour for thirty dollars, then decided it was break time. He wanted to play. The boardwalks over the bluffs leading down to the river would be getting icy by now, good sledding conditions. He'd go home, tank up on hot chocolate, then hit the boards.

"Little boy! Little boy!"

Adam looked around. A front door was open just wide enough for a very old lady to stick out her head. Her hair and skin were so white, he could barely make out her face against the snow.

"Little boy, are you looking for shoveling work?"

"Actually," said Adam, "I'm quitting."

"Good," said the old lady. "I like a boy who never quits. You'll do my house?"

Adam tried again but could see this was hopeless. The lady had to be deaf as a post. In a loud voice, he said he'd been shoveling for hours and was FINISHED and she told him how much she'd loved visiting Helsinki.

He surveyed the driveway and walk. Not even a footprint. He felt like running away. But what if she couldn't get out to go to the supermarket? What if she starved to death? It would be all his fault.

"Delighted to meet you," the old lady said. "What's your name?"

"ADAM," he shouted. It felt good to scream at her.

"Benjamin?" she said. "That's my son's name, too. You remind me of him. He lives in New York. He's sixty-four."

Adam smiled weakly and started shoveling out the end of the driveway, where big chunks of snow had been piled high by the street plows. He was trying to think pleasant thoughts, and there were plenty, considering all he'd missed with school being canceled. No math chapter test. No baritone horn lesson. No before-school/after-school voluntary/mandatory test-prep class for the state exams. No Quiz Bowl Gladiator meet—he wondered if they'd make it up or cancel it. He didn't even mind missing basketball practice. The one nice thing about being the most overprogrammed middle-school kid in America was that doing nothing felt like a special treat. Even shoveling snow seemed enjoyable.

No way Adam was checking his e-mail when he got home. He knew there'd be at least ten messages from Jennifer, about stuff they had to do for the next issue of the *Slash,* Harris Elementary/Middle School's student newspaper. They had planned a big story meeting that afternoon for the February issue — right about now, actually. Jennifer was so hard-core, she'd probably schedule a makeup meeting at her house tonight. Sorry, Jennifer. Could he help it if his e-mail was down?

He heard something and looked up. He hadn't noticed, but an SUV had stopped nearby and some big kids were hopping out and coming toward him.

One said something. Adam didn't hear the whole comment, but it sounded like they were trying to ask about shoveling jobs. He wished they'd come twenty minutes earlier; he gladly would have given them this job.

"Making much?" one said.

Adam nodded. "Lot of snow," he said.

"Give me your money," the kid said.

"I know that kid," another boy said.

Adam looked at the second boy, who was smaller. Why did they want his money? That was weird. Out of the corner of his eye, he saw a quick movement—an arm?—and there was a sharp flash of pain in the middle of his face. He felt dizzy, then nauseous. His breath smelled sour and he gagged. He didn't want to throw up in front of these kids.

His sweatshirt hood was yanked over his head, and someone had him in a bear hug from behind and was going through his pockets. They shoved him into a snowbank. Car doors slammed. By the time he got to his feet, the dark SUV was at the end of the street.

Adam was supposed to go around back and leave his wet stuff by the furnace, but he walked in the front door. His mother opened her mouth, then stopped. "What happened?" she asked.

"You need to call someone," Adam said, "to finish shoveling on Marlboro Street. An old lady could die of starvation."

"Your nose is bleeding," she said.

"Yeah," said Adam. "A kid hit me."

"Hit you?" said his mother. "Why?"

"I don't know," said Adam. "I didn't do anything to them. They took my money."

"Oh, my God," she said. "You've been mugged."

Mugged, Adam thought. He hadn't been mugged. They just hit him and took his money. His mom got a washcloth and cleaned his face. She kept asking questions, then went into the kitchen. She was calling the police? It was only forty dollars, not some big deal.

Within ten minutes three police cars had arrived. "The benefit of living in a suburb where nothing ever happens," said his mom as she watched them come up the walk. Six officers filled the Canfields' living room. They looked huge to Adam. Each had a gun strapped in a holster. His mother talked to them, then they wanted to ask Adam questions.

He told them what he remembered and one wrote it down on some kind of report sheet. Adam felt like he was watching this happen to somebody else. They kept asking the same questions. He wasn't sure how many boys there were, he told them, but more than two. He wasn't sure how old; they looked like high school. The police asked him to describe the car.

"SUV," said Adam. "Like a Ford Explorer. Like, black."

"Sure it was an Explorer?" the officer asked. "Not a Tahoe? They're pretty close."

Adam wasn't sure.

"So a black SUV the size of an Explorer?" said the cop who was filling out the report. "Not navy blue or midnight charcoal, right?"

"I'm not sure," said Adam. "A dark color, though."

"You didn't get the license plate?"

He thought he remembered AK3 something, something, something, 5.

The police kept asking if there was any bad blood with these kids from school. "Tell me again," said one. "What did they say?"

"Almost nothing," said Adam. "Just give them the money. And one kid said he knew me."

"OK," said the cop, looking up from the paper and staring directly at Adam. "And did you know him?"

"Yeah," said Adam. "Kenny Gilbert. I don't really know him, but I know who he is. I played soccer with him a few years ago in the Tremble Rec league. He was older. It was my first year. He played A line; I was on B. I play A now."

"You sure?" said the cop.

"Oh yeah," said Adam. "I'm one of the best now; I always play A line."

"That it was this Kenny Gilbert?" said the cop.

Adam nodded.

His mother found the skinny phone book that had listings for their town. "There are two Gilberts," she said, handing the book to an officer. He studied the names, and asked to borrow the book; then all the cops left.

Within thirty minutes one car was back. The police said they had the kid and needed Adam to make an ID.

Adam and his mother rode in the backseat of the police car. What Adam remembered most — besides his mom holding his hand the whole way — was that you couldn't open the doors or roll down the windows from the patrol car's backseat.

They drove a few miles, then turned onto a side street. The houses looked normal — not rich, not poor. Up ahead, he saw two police cars double-parked in the center of the block. The car Adam was in stopped one house before them.

The policeman driving Adam did not turn off the engine. He did not ask Adam to get out. "They're going to walk this kid to the sidewalk and have him stand there. I want you to look at him real good and make sure it's him. He doesn't know you're ID'ing him, and he won't be able to see you from here. He'll be looking straight ahead."

Adam waited. The front door of the house opened, and a detective in a navy-blue Windbreaker with TREMBLE POLICE in big yellow letters on the back came out, a boy standing beside him. A woman stayed behind, at the front door — probably the kid's mom — and while she waited, Adam noticed that she checked the mailbox.

The boy reached the sidewalk and stopped, standing kind of slouchy. People in nearby houses peeked out from behind curtains and blinds.

The police officer turned to Adam in the back-seat. "That him?" the officer asked.

Adam nodded.

"You sure, kid?"

"Sure," said Adam.

The officer picked up a handheld radio, pressed a button, and said, "We have a confirmation from the victim."

chapter 2

Way Below the Surface

That's fifty-eight, Adam counted to himself. Or was it fifty-seven? Normally Adam couldn't wait to get his seventy-five laps done. Swimming was his least favorite sport. He'd been known to cheat at practice. Pull himself along with the lane dividers when the coaches weren't looking. Touch his feet on the bottom and walk-swim. Count two laps for every one.

But this morning, he was in no hurry. He liked having his head underwater. He wanted to be someplace where no one asked questions.

He touched again, and thought he heard someone calling his name. That never happened at Saturday practice. Getting in the pool at 7:30 A.M., everyone was dazed; the coaches could go the entire two hours without saying a word. Adam broke stroke just enough to peek up. Oh, cripes — even with his goggles on, he recognized those long brown feet, their red-painted toenails wiggling in flip-flops. Jennifer! The girl was indefatigable. He tumbled into a flip turn so deep, his belly scraped bottom.

Jennifer! Didn't she ever get worn down? The combined December/January issue of the *Slash* had just come out last week, and all she wanted to do was talk about what was going to be in the February issue. Adam could not take it. He did not have the endurance to be coeditor of the *Slash* with Jennifer. They filled one issue, but there was no time to enjoy it; the very next morning he woke up and there was a ton of fresh news to worry about.

He'd been so proud of the last issue, especially the lead story on the resignation of Mrs. Marris as Harris principal. Adam had caught her red-handed stealing $75,000 of the school's money, and once they printed it in the *Slash,* she was fired. They called the paper the *Slash,* after the slash mark in Harris Elementary/Middle School, but Adam liked to think that their pens were so mighty, they slashed like swords through thick, swampy lies until they reached the truth.

Slash! Sammy, the *Slash*'s undercover food critic, exposed problems with the cafeteria mashed potatoes in a groundbreaking investigation. It was Adam and Jennifer's story in the *Slash* that had saved all the basketball hoops in Tremble County. And thanks to the *Slash,* kids at Harris learned that the new acting principal would be Mrs. Quigley before many teachers knew.

Mrs. Quigley. Adam repeated the name to himself as he went into another flip turn. A very liquidy name. Adam worried she might be like Marris, another mortal enemy of the *Slash.* He wondered if she was going to battle them on every story they wrote, like Marris, and if they'd have to investigate her, too. At the very least, he figured she was a nut job; she'd insisted on having her photo taken hugging the school.

Heading to the wall, Adam spotted those two long feet, this time kicking up a storm of bubbles. Jennifer would want to know what he had for the February issue.

With every stroke he heard her; she must be

running along the side of the pool, screaming. Too bad for Jennifer—everyone knew it was impossible to hear underwater.

Only the blast of the lifeguard's whistle made him stop.

He stood and pushed up his goggles—just in time to see Jennifer hand the whistle back to the lifeguard. "You didn't hear me yelling?" she asked.

"You can't hear underwater," he said. "I had to finish my seventy-five laps."

"Seventy-five?" she said. "I counted a hundred and two. You're the only one left."

Adam looked around. Whoa, even the coaches were gone. He'd really been in a fog.

"You didn't get my e-mails?" Jennifer asked.

"Computer's down," Adam said.

Jennifer shot him a look. Adam really was awful at lying, which she was normally able to twist to her advantage. "Not a problem—we'll walk over and use the library computers," she said. "I don't know about you, but I have to research my science project. And it's a quiet place to talk about the February *Slash*."

"I really can't," said Adam. "I have to—"

Jennifer was staring. "Your nose!" she said.

He'd forgotten for a minute. "It's nothing. Hit it on the boardwalk sledding."

"It's fat as a banana," she said. "Let me see."

"Please, no," Adam said, pulling away. "I didn't turn quick enough, hit a boardwalk post. Anyway, I can't go to the library; my mom's picking me up. We're doing errands."

"Not a problem," said Jennifer. "When you didn't e-mail, I called your mom. She said it was fine to go to the library and even thanked me, because my dad's driving us home."

Adam felt like Robert E. Lee in the social studies unit on the Civil War. Ulysses S. Jennifer had him surrounded.

"Your mom sounds worried," Jennifer went on. "She said, 'Jen, be nice to him; he had a tough day yesterday.'"

"What'd she mean by that?" Adam snapped.

"She didn't say," answered Jennifer. "I guess she meant the sledding accident."

Adam nodded. He felt relieved. He'd made his parents promise not to tell anyone. The last thing he wanted was to be known as the idiot who got his shoveling money stolen.

They were almost to the locker rooms when

Adam noticed—Jennifer wasn't wet. "Didn't you even go swimming?" he asked.

"Just put on a bathing suit. You need one to get on the pool deck. I hate pools in winter. I freeze."

"Really," Adam said.

He was impressed—for a skinny person, Jennifer made a huge splash.

As she bobbed up, she looked outraged. The lifeguard was blowing his whistle and yelling, "You do that again and you're out of here."

"Sorry," Adam said. "My arm slipped." The fact was, he'd had no choice.

He offered Jennifer a hand up, but she spit water in his face. So he hurried to the locker room, fast-walking instead of running. He didn't want to get whistled at again.

Even on a Saturday morning after a big snow, the Tremble children's library—on the second floor of the main branch—was crowded. Instead of getting a table by the young adult section, Adam and Jennifer were lucky to find one near the picture books.

Jennifer pulled a thick stack of printouts from her backpack.

"Geez," said Adam. "Looks pretty scientific."

"Yeah," she said. "My dad showed me how to run nitrate levels for these river samples. He set up this program for me—makes it a lot easier. This won't take long," she said, and headed off to find a computer.

Adam hadn't quite got his science project going. His dad gave him a few ideas that he'd written up as abstracts, but they seemed boring. He'd come up with something—the fair was still a few months away.

He pulled out the paperback they were reading for language arts but could not concentrate. The words were wiggly. Each line reminded him of a lap at the pool. He kept thinking: Would those creeps come after him for calling the police?

Little kids were doing puzzles or playing with the library's collection of plastic dinosaurs. Adam used to love coming with his dad on Saturday mornings. Library dinosaurs were big and fierce, bright purple and green and yellow, made of hard plastic. In the Quiet Corner, a father was sitting with two little boys, reading to them. Adam missed big picture books with one large drawing on every page and just a couple of words. Little kids had a great life. No worries.

"Doing lots of reading?" Jennifer asked, flopping her nitrate printouts onto the table. When Adam didn't answer, she gently tapped him on the head with a yellow pad—the list of story ideas for the February *Slash*. "Anyone home?" she said. "Adam, you are even more spacey than usual. You OK?"

Adam nodded.

"So, I've got this easy story that will cover us for Black History Month," Jennifer said. "Tremble County is going to rename a street for Martin Luther King. Isn't that perfect? A feel-good story." Adam knew the street; it was in the Willows, the poorest and most heavily black section of the county. "They're having a bunch of kids from Harris go to some rainbow ceremony. Sound good?"

Adam nodded.

"I'd be glad to do it."

Adam nodded.

Sammy was finishing a story rating the best egg-bacon-and-cheese sandwiches. "He's visited five delis so far," she said. "He's got seven to go. He says it's pretty interesting—some fry the eggs, some scramble them, and there's a lot of subtleties. He'll score each sandwich from one to four yummy-yummies. Okey-dokey?"

Adam nodded.

Their sports feature was a look at the girls' volley-ball team. And they were planning a brief story listing the distinguished guests coming for the Say No to Drugs Community Players pageant—basically every politician in Tremble County.

"Phoebe's got a bunch of stuff," Jennifer said.

Adam nodded. He wasn't surprised. Phoebe, third-grade phenom.

"She seems to be on this big environment kick," Jennifer said. "You know Phoebe. Slightly obsessed. They made her recycling captain for third grade. I think she wants to use it as a springboard to higher office. She supports capital punishment for kids who throw a juice can in the regular trash. She says she got this great front-page idea at recycling club. . . . Where is it?" Jennifer rifled through a pile of notes. "Here. Something about a three-hundred-year-old tree being cut down. She says it's an outrage. It didn't sound that interesting, but . . ."

"But she *really* wanted to do it?" Adam said, his voice a whisper.

"How'd you know?" Jennifer said, smiling, but Adam did not smile back.

"There's a school board meeting coming up," she continued. "I know you hate meetings, but I think we should go. A lot of the most annoying stuff they do to us gets started at board meetings." Jennifer braced for a fight, but Adam just nodded. She'd never seen him in such an agreeable, nodding mood. They were getting lots done.

She asked how his investigation of the school science fair was going. For weeks Adam had been telling Jennifer he was set to unleash this *huge* story about how parents were the real ones doing kids' science projects.

"Any chance you'll have it for February?" she asked.

Adam nodded.

"Great," said Jennifer.

"I mean no," said Adam. "I was nodding no."

"OK," said Jennifer, making a note. "Sorry I got that nod upside down."

Adam nodded.

"Sooo, I rescheduled the staff meeting for Monday." She paused. "Adam, do you have anything for February? We could use a front-pager from you."

Adam nodded. They always wanted the big ones from him. Just once in his lousy life, couldn't he do an easy story? Something that wouldn't piss people off, something positive and heartwarming? People assumed that because he did investigations, he liked to pick fights. They assumed that if he got rid of one principal, that's what he did for a living. Already kids were asking him if he had any dirt on Quigley.

"Would you like an idea?" Jennifer asked. "See if you like this. I got an e-mail. This lady wants to give us an exclusive. Not an entire exclusive, she said—a local exclusive. She's a press representative for a big *Gentleman's World* reporter, Erik Forrest. He's written for all the top newspapers—*New York Times, Wall Street Journal, Washington Post.* You ever hear of him? Well, he's covered wars and Princess Di and a bunch of famous murder trials. And now he's got a new book coming out and he'll be at the mall bookstore and they said they'd give us a one-on-one."

Jennifer waited, but Adam didn't even nod. "I thought, you know, you're a great reporter, and he's a great reporter; you'd have lots to talk about. My dad has some of his old war books and he says the guy's great. I brought them for you. And the press people sent his new one. Sound OK?"

She handed him the books. "Adam, say some-thing. You're scaring me."

"When's your father coming?" he said.

When Adam got home, his mom and dad hugged him and took his coat and swim bag and together they made him lunch. And neither read the paper while he ate. They kept asking questions about swim-ming and the library and the books he'd brought home, as if he'd just had the most interesting morn-ing in the world.

After he said for the third time that he didn't want dessert, they led him into the living room to "discuss" a few things.

A Tremble police detective had called. Besides this kid Kenny Gilbert, they had picked up four more boys. Adam was amazed there were that many, but the police said a couple had stayed inside the SUV the whole time. His mom read off the names. Adam didn't recognize any. This was fabulous—now it was five kids who'd want to kill him.

And that wasn't all. His mother said it was prob-ably going to be on the news. They couldn't stop it. She said the police had put out a press release.

"For a forty-dollar robbery?" Adam said.

"It's not the money," said his dad. "It's the idea: 'Kid Mugged for His Shoveling Money! In the Suburbs!' You're a newshound, Adam. You know people eat up that stuff. Plus, the arrests were made so fast—makes it look like the Tremble police are right on top of things."

Adam felt dizzy and let his head plop against the sofa.

"My name?" he said.

"No, no, no," said his dad. "They wouldn't release that. You're a minor. We said absolutely not. No one will know."

Adam looked at his father. Did grown-ups live on the same planet? "Right, Dad," said Adam. "No one will know." He headed up to his room. He said he just needed to lie down for a minute.

When he woke, it was Sunday morning.

chapter 3

Bully News

The all-news radio station slogan was, "Give us twenty minutes and we'll give you the world," and all day Sunday, Adam's bloody nose was apparently one of the biggest stories in the entire world. "A sordid snow shoveling tragedy," they called it. Boland Action News 12 promised "All News All the Time," and like clockwork at seven minutes past the hour, an anchorwoman who'd been smiling just seconds before turned deadly serious, looked into the camera, and began, "Is there any place where our children are safe?" And every hour she said it, she misted up at precisely seven past, as if she and Adam were dear friends and she was barely able to go on living.

Even the Tri-River Region's big city papers ran stories. One headline read, "Newest Outrage: Mugged for His Shoveling Money!"

The news accounts made the whole thing sound so much larger and more important than it had felt to Adam. They said he'd been "assaulted by five teenagers joyriding in a late-model SUV." They said he'd been left "beaten in a snowdrift." They gave the boys' names and said they would be charged with felony assault and robbery, which carried prison sentences of up to four years.

They did not give Adam's name. But they said that the "victim"—they used that word about ten times per sentence—was a middle-school student who was jumped by the "vile predators" in Tremble's River Path section.

He hadn't felt so awful about going to school since the day he and Jennifer had come out with the story about Mrs. Marris stealing the money. Why didn't those vile predators have the decency to hurt him someplace he could hide under his shirt? From inside,

26

his nose didn't feel too bad, but from the outside it was as purple and yellow as a library dinosaur.

Wherever he went, he kept his head down. If friends passed in the hall, he'd wave but yell that he was late — a very believable excuse in Adam's case — and keep right on going.

He took lunch in the library, alone. He got to his classes early and sat right down, pretending he was working. After school, he stayed in a bathroom stall for fifteen minutes doing math homework. He planned to walk into the newsroom after the *Slash* meeting started. The last thing he wanted was to give a roomful of reporters the chance to conduct a press conference about his nose.

And he was surprised. It didn't seem like anyone knew. At least no one said anything. It had taken a lot of bobbing and weaving, but he'd faked out the school. Maybe he'd overblown things. Who cared, really?

Adam opened the door to Room 306 quietly. He ducked his head and tiptoed along the far wall to the back of the newsroom. He'd never felt so stealth-like. When he looked up, they were all staring.

At *him.*

When he stared back, they immediately gazed at the floor, the ceiling, any place but Adam.

He made eye contact with Jennifer, who was standing up front. "We were just talking about stories for February," she said.

"That's good," said Adam. "Sorry, I'm late, I was just—"

"No problem," said Jennifer. "Really, don't worry about it. We didn't get that far."

Adam nodded. "What are you up to?"

Now Jennifer was looking at the floor.

"The staff feels we need to do a story on . . . ah . . . well . . . see . . . um . . . *bullies.* . . . Not special ones, just bullies in general. Regular bullies. You know, random bullies."

"Random bullies," Adam repeated. Did they . . . ? Had they figured . . . ? Please, no.

"We're sick of it!" said a typist, and now they were all talking at once, competing to tell the most gruesome bully stories. There were back-of-the-school-bus bully stories, bathroom bully stories, bully stories about purposely being hit in the face with a dodgeball in gym.

"So here's my idea," Jennifer said, and she told

them about this famous newspaper, the *Village Voice,* that she'd read about on the Romenesko journalism website. For years the paper did an annual exposé on the ten worst New York City slumlords—landlords who didn't care if their apartment buildings turned into rat-infested dumps.

"We could do the ten worst bullies at Harris Elementary/Middle School," Jennifer said.

Ten worst bullies? They loved it! People were bouncing on couches, banging computers, standing on tables for the chance to nominate their favorite bully.

Except Adam. He felt sick.

He couldn't believe how carried away they were getting. He had to stop this. Everyone at school would know. They'd assume he ordered up the story because of the snow-shoveling mess. They'd think it was his pathetic way of getting back at his bullies.

"Excuse me," he said weakly. "Excuse me." They would not quiet down. "Can I talk for one minute?" It made him mad. All the frustration of the last few days was welling up inside. Bullies? What did they know about bullies? He had to make them listen.

Adam grabbed his backpack and hurled it against the wall so hard that a bulletin board full of *Slash* citations for excellence crashed to the floor. Citations floated across the room.

Everyone turned toward him.

"Thanks for the chance to talk," he began. "I'm only the coeditor around here."

"Ad-man, you know we love you," said Sammy.

"Yeah, yeah," said Adam. "And you know, no one loves kicking butt more than I do. Guys, don't forget, I was the number-one person behind Sammy's groundbreaking investigation of the cafeteria mashed potatoes. And I *did* help get Marris fired as principal. So, I'm not afraid of trouble. But I see a big problem." He paused. "You want top ten bullies? Tell me how we rank them. How do we decide what makes one bully worse than another? There's no fair way. Is a kid who bangs your head against the bus window worse than a kid who grabs you and whispers, 'How's it going, fat boy?'"

"Adam," said Jennifer, "Adam, listen—"

"Is a kid who pushes you off your bike worse than a kid who gives you a wedgie?"

"Adam," Jennifer said. "Let me—"

He was hot. "Is a kid who shoots his grandmother and buries her in the basement worse than a kid who dumps her in a cement mixer?"

"ADAM!" shouted Jennifer. "STOP! PLEASE! Look, I agree. Newspapers must be fair. But you're talking about problems that would come up if *we,* the *Slash* staff, decide on the worst bullies—if *we* try to set up our own point system and *we* rank the bullies and *we* serve as the total judge of bulliness. But we don't have to do that. What if we run a poll? We announce it on the front page of the February issue. Every kid at Harris gets to vote for the worst bully. And then we print the bully poll results in March."

Even when Jennifer was wrong, she talked better than he did. He could see her idea racing happily through their sloshy brains. First one, then several said it was a great plan, and Sammy the food critic shouted, "Bully poll!" and they were all chanting, "Bully poll! Bully poll!"

Adam put up his hands. "OK," he said. "If we're going to list the ten worst bullies, we have to give them a chance to give their side, right? That's the fairness rule. So, you're going to have to ask them how it feels being a top ten bully—and they're going to pound you out. Remember: they're bullies. We're not talking Billys—*bullies*!"

Jennifer would not back down. "Kids might actually be happy making the list," she said. "Like they're the most feared or toughest. It won't be that bad."

Ulysses S. Jennifer was not going to surround him again. He had to make them feel fear, quick. "All right," he said. "Just one favor. Before we announce the poll in the *Slash,* we need to find out which of you will volunteer to talk to the top ten bullies. I need a list of people willing to interview the bullies and get the bully side of the story. People who don't mind going face-to-face with the most vicious kids at school. It'd probably be good if you know karate. Or if your parents are paramedics for an ambulance service or are licensed to use a defibrillator. Let's see hands. I need names."

He scanned the room. They finally got it. He could see those brains focusing: they were envisioning themselves getting the crap beat out of them. Not a hand went up. Kids were staring at their feet. Kids who'd been walking around with untied shoelaces since kindergarten were suddenly bending down to tie them.

Then a measly third-grade hand shot up. Phoebe! Adam closed his eyes. This couldn't be happening. Phoebe!

"I'll do it," she squeaked. "This is a big story, all

right. I wouldn't be surprised if it wins the Pulitzer Prize gold medal for public service. Jennifer is right. It's not just a list of worst bullies for kids to laugh at. It should be required reading for grown-ups, too. Especially teacher grown-ups. They forget about us being bullied every single day of our life. Since I was in Miss Hickey's first grade, kids mocked me for being smart. 'How'd you get the answer so fast, smart girl?' And I didn't know what to say, because my mommy, she was always so proud of my smartness—I was her little smarty-pants. The way these kids said it, being the smart girl didn't sound good. They just wanted me to give them answers. And when I finally said no, they got mean. They'd whisper on the way to Miss Hickey's desk or the pencil sharpener— *Dweebie Phoebe. Phoeb the Feeb.* Where was Miss Hickey? How could that lady not hear for a whole year? Once I stayed after to talk to her. 'You're too sensitive, Phoebe.' It's not my fault! I didn't ask to be this smart so soon. And I hate them for being mean to a person who can't help it if she has high reading comprehension."

Jennifer was hurrying toward Phoebe. Everyone knew what could happen if the third grader got on one of her nervous talking streaks, like that night at the boathouse before the big exposé last semester. Jennifer had to get to her quick, put her arm around her, rub her back, calm Phoebe down, before . . .

"We have to do this," Phoebe went on. "We must say no to bullies. No bullies! We all know that one of our *Slash* coeditors—I'm not supposed to say his name—was viciously beaten by the worst bullies. . . ."

There was a gasp.

Everyone looked at Adam.

Jennifer was rubbing Phoebe's back, but it was too little, too late. "Phoebe," Jennifer moaned.

"I know," said Phoebe. "I didn't mean to; it slipped out."

"Adam, wait," Jennifer called. "Adam, come on." When he didn't slow down, she ran after him. Adam was fast, but he had a full backpack and Jennifer caught him by the door to the down stairwell.

"I've got basketball practice," he mumbled.

"You knew people were going to figure it out," she said.

"Everybody knows?" he asked.

"No," Jennifer said. "Some. The *Slash* staff—you know, reporters."

Adam started to ask how many people Jennifer had blabbed to, but stopped. This wasn't Jennifer's fault. "How long?" he asked.

"Tomorrow the rest'll probably know," she said. "That's my guess. Parents saw the news; kids saw your nose, but kids don't listen to the news. I figure when everyone gets home tonight, the lightbulbs will flash on all over town."

Adam nodded. He felt like the basketball that time his dad backed the van over it.

"You know, Adam, you can't keep news down," she said. "Marris couldn't. Even the president can't."

Adam didn't say anything.

"Are you mad about the Top Ten Bully List?" Jennifer asked.

Adam shook his head.

"We have to stand up to people like that," she said. "If you let them get away with it, they keep coming at you, like Phoebe said."

Adam nodded.

"You nervous about those creeps?" Jennifer asked.

"Nah," said Adam, looking away. "It's just five high-school kids."

chapter 4

Meeting Strange Adults

Jennifer was right. Lightbulbs did flash on all over town.

The Canfields' phone kept ringing. Adam didn't want to talk to a soul, but the calls weren't for him anyway. They were from friends of Adam's parents, who wanted to ask if he was all right. They kept saying how sorry they were, how shocked they were, how they'd wished they'd known it was Adam—they would have called sooner. Was there anything the family needed? Food? Bandages? Were they monitoring Adam's electrolyte levels? Did they need to borrow a hospital gurney?

From news reports they assumed he was near death; they couldn't believe it was just a bruised nose.

Several said how brave he'd been to fight off five hooligans single-handedly.

The detective overseeing the case also called. He suggested Adam go to the doctor. When Adam's dad said that didn't seem necessary, the detective explained that it would be good for the case if Adam needed medical attention. "Juries notice those nice details," the detective said.

The detective explained that in these situations it was common for the judge to issue a protective order so that the five accused were prohibited from having contact with the victim. "You should hear from the court soon," he said.

Adam got several e-mails from friends who all basically said the same thing: That was you, wasn't it?

He answered only one, to his grown-up friend Danny, who worked at the Tremble Animal Shelter. Danny was the rare and miraculous adult who actually seemed to understand kids. Danny wrote, "Thinking of you, buddy. Stop by when you want to talk."

Adam answered, "Thanks, Danny. I will."

/////

The next day, kids kept asking. He knew most were trying to be nice, but he wished they'd stop. In band, the trombone player who sat closest to the baritone section whispered, "Don't worry, Ad, I got your back."

A lot of kids said they were surprised that he didn't look that bad; they sounded disappointed. In the halls, he could tell people were pointing him out.

Everyone had advice on how he should have handled it. The worst were the ones who asked why he called the police. "For forty dollars?" a girl said. "How come your father didn't just go over to their house and get the money back?" After the third time, Adam came up with a pat answer.

"Ever been mugged?" he said.

That shut them up.

In the afternoon, the head guidance counselor, Mrs. Finch, called him to her office. With her was a big man Adam had never seen before. Adam knew Mrs. Finch from their Quiz Bowl Gladiator Team. She was the team adviser — officially, the Supreme High Gladiator Chieftain. She gave Adam the official Quiz Bowl Gladiator greeting: "Hail, brave warrior! From where have you come?" Adam was supposed to say, "From the battlefield of knowledge, great chieftain," but he hated that stuff, especially with a stranger sitting there. Adam had no clue who thought up this national Quiz Bowl Gladiator racket, but it really was the most ridiculous thing he'd ever heard of.

"How're you doing, Mrs. Finch?" Adam said.

Mrs. Finch cleared her throat dramatically, then whispered, "Come on, brave gladiator."

"Fromthebattlefieldofknowledgegreatchieftain," Adam mumbled.

"Good!" said Mrs. Finch. "How are you, sweetie? Need a big hug?"

Adam liked Mrs. Finch fine. She seemed to be a nice lady. It was just, you could tell that she'd spent most of her career in elementary school guidance. She was a little overfriendly for Adam's taste.

"It's OK," said Adam. "I'm good."

"Oh, I'm going to give you one anyway," said Mrs. Finch, who at least had the decency to make it a loose hug.

She introduced Adam to the big man, Mr. Scott, the head of security for Tremble's two high schools. He had a thick neck and wide shoulders and, to

Adam, looked like a pro football player. Since being mugged, Adam was amazed at how many adults he was meeting who did jobs he'd never heard of.

Mr. Scott said he'd been "fully briefed about the tragic incident" and was there to help. He said he assumed protective orders would soon be issued by the court and that would mean zero contact—these kids couldn't even say hi to Adam. And if they did, he should let the school know immediately.

"You know these yahoos, right?" said the man.

Adam shook his head. "Just one."

"But you seen what they look like?"

Adam hadn't. He explained he'd only gotten a glance at one other kid, the boy who punched him.

"Ah," said the man, "flips and snitches, huh? Didn't know that, but doesn't surprise me." Adam looked puzzled. "Cops must have flipped that Kenny Gilbert kid you ID'd and got him to snitch on the rest," Mr. Scott explained. "Nice to have friends like that, huh?

"You ought to know what they look like," Mr. Scott continued. "Not that I think they'll come after you." He pulled out a Palm Pilot and called up each of the five names. Then he called up their photos.

"Whoa," said Adam. "You got every high-school kid on that thing?"

"Every kid in the district," Mr. Scott said. "Punks like this, you grab them, the first thing they tell you is they're someone else. We just check it right there on the spot while we got 'em by the neck. Works good. With a photo, it's hard to deny you're you."

Adam stared at the faces. They looked normal. Basic big kids. No scars, no missing teeth, no tattoos on their foreheads—you couldn't tell they were vile predators.

"Any have brothers or sisters at Harris?" Adam asked.

"We checked," said Mr. Scott. "Only one at the middle school, and you won't have trouble with him."

"You know that?" said Adam.

"He's, ah . . . the boy's retarded," said Mr. Scott.

"What Mr. Scott means," said Mrs. Finch, "is developmentally disabled."

"Right," said Mr. Scott. "Sorry, I never remember. None of these modern titles sound like what people got. I always get that developmentally disabled thing mixed up with wheelchair victims."

"That's physically challenged," Mrs. Finch corrected.

"Oh, right," said Mr. Scott, who was collecting his stuff. "Will that do it?"

Adam was sitting with his legs together, his hands in his lap, his head down, lost in thought and looking small.

"Yo, it'll be OK," said Mr. Scott. "I seen lots worse situations. Every day's a little easier. Piece of cake for a gladiator like you."

"Yeah, right," Adam said, and he stood to leave before Mrs. Finch could hug him again.

He was not done meeting strange adults. After Mrs. Finch, they marched him into the principal's office.

Normally, the Harris principal had the final review of each issue of the *Slash,* but he and Jennifer had caught a break for the January issue — Marris was gone and Mrs. Quigley was just starting. So Mr. Brooks, the world history teacher, had served as a fill-in adviser for the January *Slash,* and he thought everything they did was splendid ("from the Latin *splendidus*") except their spelling, which he thought was atrocious ("from the Latin *un-splendidus*").

Mrs. Quigley's office was on the main floor, in the back, where Miss Esther's desk used to be. Adam's eyes bugged out: behind Mrs. Quigley, the door to the Bunker—Mrs. Marris's old underground headquarters—had been sealed off with yellow police crime tape.

"Cookies?" Mrs. Quigley asked, offering a platter of Adam's favorite, Mrs. Radin's Famous Homemade Super-Chunk Buckets O' Chocolate Moisty Deluxe chocolate-chip cookies.

Mrs. Quigley said she wanted Adam to know that if any of those snow-shoveling kids gave him trouble, he could come to her. "You all right?" she asked.

Adam nodded.

"Every kid at Harris telling you what you should have done?"

Adam looked at her.

"It's awful being the center of attention for something like that—you've just got to ignore the fools and keep going."

Adam liked that, except there were so many fools who needed ignoring, it was a big job.

Mrs. Quigley seemed nice, like a jolly grand-mother type. Calmer than Marris. He was surprised. He'd never considered the possibility of a principal being nice. Adam had dreaded every meeting with Marris—she'd either smiled them into submission or screamed the daylights out of them.

"Another Moisty Deluxe?" Mrs. Quigley asked.

Adam didn't mind if he did.

"Take two," she said. "I always do."

The next thing Mrs. Quigley said really caught him off-guard. She said he'd done a terrific job on the *Slash* and that she admired how hard the staff worked. She said she believed in a free press—her dad had been a copy editor back East in Massachusetts for the *Boston Traveler* until it folded in the 1960s. She said when she graduated from college, she'd wanted to be a reporter, but it was mostly a man's business back then, so she became a teacher.

Mrs. Quigley told Adam she understood that trying to censor the *Slash* was slippery business, as Mrs. Marris had learned too late. "If the Chinese Communists can't control the Internet," she said, "it's unlikely I can control the news here in Tremble."

But she also said that trust was a two-way street and that the more famous the *Slash* became, the more people would be gunning for it and the more an error or bad judgment could cost them. "You need an adult's advice," she said, "and I'll try to be as truthful and fair as I can. But once we agree on a plan, I expect you to follow it. You get my meaning?"

Adam did. She didn't want to get kicked out of her job like Marris.

"I promise to do my best to protect you," she said. "But I warn you, they brought me out of retirement to do this, and I'm just here as acting principal. There's a chance that when the year's over, I'm gone. I've still got lots to learn — like where the bodies are buried."

Adam sneaked another look at the yellow police tape across the Bunker door.

"Not literally," she said. "At least I hope not. Anyway, I look forward to our meeting for the February issue. Got anything good working?"

Adam started to say, then stopped. This Mrs. Quigley seemed good, but after Marris, Adam wasn't sure. It was possible that her niceness was a trick. Plus one thing she'd said made him nervous.

Why did she need to protect them? Protect them from what?

Jennifer's mom, who was a big PTA honcho, stopped by a little before seven to pick up Adam for the school board meeting. Adam hated meetings. Why was he going? He'd totally lost control of his life.

It started with the pledge. Then some elementary kids sang "God Bless America," and scores of certificates were handed out for the best spellers at the annual Bolandvision Cable Bee.

Through it all, Jennifer took notes. Adam kept sneaking glances. What was she taking notes on? She had neat, looping handwriting, and she filled line after line, then page after page in an 8½-by-11-inch spiral notebook. The girl was a machine; the words kept looping out of her pen. Adam didn't have a single word written down yet. What was wrong with him?

The school board president had a question for the first-assistant-associate-superintendent: How many schools would be participating in the ceremony renaming the Willows street in honor of Dr. Martin Luther King?

The first-assistant-associate-superintendent could not, of course, just say six and sit down. The man had to show off what a genius he was. He had to remind everyone what an exciting joint venture this was between the Tremble schools and the Tremble Zoning Board, and how pages and pages of signatures

had been collected on petitions to rename the street—
"a true sign of Tremble's multicultural spirit."

He had to say exactly how many kids from each
school would be going and how many were white,
black, Hispanic, and Asian. "We might need to tweak
those numbers," said the first-assistant-associate-
superintendent, whose name was Dr. Bleepin. "Right
now we're a little heavy on Asians, a touch light on
Hispanics, but I promise a diverse group in the spirit
of Dr. King's quest for integration."

Adam had his eyes shut, and Jennifer nudged
him. "Are you asleep?" she whispered.

"Unfortunately wide awake," he said. "It's easier
to spot the lies with my eyes closed."

Adam felt like he was being tortured; this
Bleepin maniac was just warming up. "I want to add
that Mr. and Mrs. Boland and the Boland Foundation
have very generously underwritten the cost of the
entire event," Dr. Bleepin went on. "They've offered
their Bolandvision Mobile Entertainment unit and an
eighteen-wheel flatbed truck we can park right on
the street—it converts to a stage. So all the dignitaries will be able to sit very high up. And they've
hired a professional singing group, the Perfect Mix—

a music ensemble, does a lot of work in schools; you may have seen them featured on Boland News 12's Community Miracles program Sunday mornings at six. Their songs cover all Big Four ethnic flavors."

"Thank you, Dr. Bleepin," said the board president.

"In the food department," continued Dr. Bleepin, "the Boland Foundation has underwritten twelve kinds of sushi, both chicken *and* beef burritos—"

"Excellent," said the board president. "The thing is—I can't remember—did you give us a date?"

"Actually, I don't have one from the county but—"

"No date?" said the board president. "This late?"

"Oh, just a few loose ends to tie up," Dr. Bleepin said cheerfully. "We'll have it this week and send flyers home."

Adam opened his eyes. He took the notebook from his back pocket. He pulled out his pen. He held the pen top in his teeth and wrote three words in the notebook. Then he put the pen and notebook away.

Jennifer leaned over. "What?" she whispered. By now she'd filled nineteen 8½-by-11 pages. "What was it?"

"Tell you later," he whispered.

Once more that evening Adam opened his eyes, during the public forum at the end, when anyone could speak. Most of it was stuff like how great the crossing guards were. A few were nut cases, and Adam found them the most interesting—if you listened carefully, there was usually a nugget of truth.

One woman identified herself as an outraged single mother. She was complaining about homework being unfair to young kids who don't have parents at home to help. Adam tried imagining a world without homework, but the closest he could get was a field full of kids looking at the clouds. This woman was not going to convince anyone, he was sure.

Then she said something about the science fair that made him open his eyes. He didn't make a note right then; he waited for her to finish.

Jennifer watched. Adam walked to the rear of the auditorium, crossed to the other side, and then went down the row to where Outraged Single Mother sat. He leaned over to her, said something, and gave her his notebook. She wrote in it.

On the way home, Jennifer's mom paid them no mind; she had on her headset and was making calls.

They were sitting in the Astro van's backseat,

and Jennifer had put on the overhead light. "So, what'd you write down?" she asked.

Adam opened his notebook. There were about five words. Near the top he'd written, "King/No Date."

"Something's going on with renaming that street in the Willows for Dr. King," Adam said.

"What?" said Jennifer.

"You don't feel it?" Adam said. "That Bleepin idiot — he knows the shoe size of every Spanish kid going to the ceremony but doesn't know the date?"

Jennifer was quiet. "I see what you're saying," she said. "So what do I do? Call him up?"

"If you want six more notebooks of lies," said Adam.

"My mom's the one who told me," said Jennifer. "She heard about it at a PTA meeting. She thought it was wonderful."

Adam nodded. "No offense, but PTA people — they look for the best in their fellow humans."

"Wait," said Jennifer. "What about that woman you met in the Willows? The one who helped you on the Marris story? What was her name?"

"Mrs. Willard," Adam said.

"You said she knew everything about the Willows. She might know."

Adam shrugged.

Jennifer peeked at his pad again. "What's this?"

"Outraged Single Mother's phone number," he said.

"You want to do a story about no homework?"

"No," said Adam. "It's for my science fair investigation. It tees me off, how much parents do the projects."

"Wait," said Jennifer. "Your parents don't help? I remember you guys couldn't go to your grandma's cottage on spring vacation last year 'cause you were all getting your project done."

"Me, too," Adam said. "But I can't stop thinking about this one thing. You remember last year—the rows on the far side of the gym?"

Jennifer did. Everyone in the middle school had to do a project, and the far sides were mostly kids in low classes. A lot of those projects were wobbly posters Scotch-taped together; their hypotheses and conclusions were handwritten and crooked. It didn't look like they'd gotten lots of help.

"So what do you do?" asked Jennifer. "Not have a science fair?"

"I don't know," said Adam. "I just figured Outraged Single Mother might give me an idea."

The Astro van pulled up to his house. He undid his seatbelt, opened the sliding door, and hopped out.

"You OK?" she asked. "You were pretty quiet tonight."

Adam shrugged and closed the door.

chapter 5

Sir Isaac

With twenty minutes left in science class, Mr. Devillio said, "Let's take a break from the excretory system and hear how those science projects are coming along. I know you're thinking it's late January and the fair's months away, but it sneaks up on you. You start, young lady."

Young lady. Typical Devillio, Adam thought. More than halfway through the school year and the man was calling them "young lady" or "son." He still didn't know their names.

The girl explained that she was studying the relationship between kids' weight and the number of times they ate at fast-food restaurants per month, but Adam doubted Devillio heard a word—he appeared to be scrolling through the e-mails on his BlackBerry.

Adam had never seen a teacher with such a high phony quotient—the ratio between what grown-ups think of a teacher and what kids know. Adults treated him like Sir Isaac Devillio. The man taught all the honors science classes, was chairman of the middle-school science department, ran the Harris science fair and the county science fair, and constantly reminded Adam's class of all the high muckety-muck state committees he served on. It seemed like every time Adam picked up the local paper, the *Citizen-Gazette-Herald-Advertiser,* there was Mr. Devillio shaking some high and mighty hand.

But teaching? Adam never had such a boring teacher. And so lazy. Devillio was constantly late to class, and then he'd spend forever telling them about his car troubles, his migraine headaches, his swollen ankles, his canker sore.

On the other hand, when Adam was late—automatic detention. No excuses, son.

"You're next, son." A boy was going to calculate

whether a baseball traveled farther when hit by an aluminum or wooden bat.

Day after day, Mr. Devillio drilled them on the definitions in their study packets. "Son, give me the three basic parts of the nephron."

"Who knows the seven materials filtered out of the blood by the Bowman's capsule? I guarantee, it'll be on the state test."

He never finished a packet, so his tests were full of questions that they never covered. But if they complained? "You know you are responsible for everything in those packets."

Teachers were not supposed to use cell phones in school, but Mr. Devillio told Adam's class he had a special waiver because of all his "indispensable" committee work, and he repeatedly left the room to take calls. When he returned, he forgot what he'd been teaching and repeated himself. A boy in their class had made the mistake of trying to correct Mr. Devillio. "We just did the three parts and two functions of the circulatory system," the boy said. "I think we're supposed to be up to the three types of cells in plasma."

"Oh, you know everything about the three parts

and two functions—is that right, son? Then let's have the test right now."

After that, they let him repeat himself.

The next project was running mice through a maze and testing whether different kinds of music made the mice go faster. Adam walked up to the wastebasket to toss out a tissue; he noticed that Mr. Devillio appeared to be Googling Chinese restaurants in West Tremble.

Adam was sure Devillio never read the papers he had them write on every unit. Adam had done an eight-pager on the circulatory system, and the only comment Devillio put on it was on the bibliography, taking off points because Adam had forgotten to list a book's date of publication.

It hadn't been Adam who nicknamed Mr. Devillio the Devil, but Adam totally agreed with it.

Before Mr. Devillio could call on another student, there was a low buzzing sound they all recognized. The girl sitting behind Adam leaned forward and whispered, "The Devil's vibrating."

"Did someone say something?" asked Mr. Devillio, scanning the room for a victim, and at the same time, pulling out his cell phone. He squinted at the number display. "The state high commission on standards. Everyone wants a piece of me. I don't know how I do it. All right, you're next, young lady. I'll be listening from my office," he said, going out and closing the door.

The girl started describing her project, but every other word, some kid made a fake cough that sounded like "boring" or "stupid" or stuff from a bull's excretory system.

Adam decided to go for it; no way the Devil could hear them through that door. "Hey," he called in a loud whisper. "I got a quick question. Come on. How many of you get help at home on the science fair? I know it sounds stupid, but there's a reason."

They looked at one another. Adam raised his own hand, then a few hands went up, then all of them.

"Why're you asking?" said a girl. "You know everyone's parents always help."

Adam shook his head. "Not everyone," he said. "Everyone in *here.*"

The office door opened, and Adam froze, but Jennifer began talking, smooth and controlled, like she'd been describing her project for the last ten minutes. She was babbling about nitrates being dumped into the river and stimulating annoying weed growth. She said she was trying to figure out if the problem was discharge from the sewage treatment plant upriver or fertilizers washing off the golf course and people's lawns.

"Sounds fine, young lady," said Mr. Devillio. "I'm pleased to hear—"

Adam raised his hand. He was sick of holding back. Maybe that's what was wrong with him lately. He needed to take action. Be more like the old Adam, who brought down a principal.

"What is it, son?"

"Mr. Devillio," he said. "There's something I want to ask about the science fair. I know it's really great and everything, but I think it's kind of . . . well, not fair that certain kids get tons of help at home and some kids—"

"Parents helping on projects?" Mr. Devillio said. "Parents helping?" He walked back around his desk, the whole time saying, "Parents helping?" Adam wasn't fooled. He knew Devillio was stalling so he could get the seating chart and figure out who Adam was.

"Well . . . Adam," he said. "Yes, Adam, do you know cases of parents helping? Because if you do, Adam, I want to hear now." He held up a clipboard and pen. "Give me names, Adam. I'll put a stop to it immediately. I'll make calls home tonight. You all know you can get help at the after-school sessions I hold every week."

Kids were staring at their desks. Anyone who ever went to one of those sessions knew how useless they were. There were so many kids, you were lucky to get a minute with the man. Half the time he was on his stupid cell phone. And then all he did was give you a book to look for ideas in or a website to go to.

Mr. Devillio stopped at Adam's desk. "Now, Adam," he said in a loud voice. "Adam! Look at me! Adam, are your parents helping on your project? Are they?"

Adam looked down.

Mr. Devillio took his clipboard and smacked the desktop so hard, Adam popped out of his seat.

"Answer me, son," the teacher yelled. "Answer me!"

Still staring at his desk, Adam shook his head and in a barely audible voice, said, "No."

The bell rang.

"Well, good," said Mr. Devillio. "From now on, you just worry about yourself, Adam Copperfield. That should keep you plenty busy."

Adam picked up his book, slid his excretory materials into the binder, then jammed it all into his backpack.

As kids crowded out, several made comments under their breath. "Moron," they whispered. "Loser." Even Jennifer gave him a look that said, Have you lost your mind?

What *had* he been thinking? He had to get out of that room. His face felt flushed. He tried pushing past the logjam of kids at the door and into the hallway, but the mob moved at its own pace. Sweat was trickling down his back, dripping down his temples. The Devil's room was a million degrees.

That afternoon, Adam went right home after school. He skipped Geography Challenge. He skipped basketball practice. He told the nurse he had a stomachache.

It was a lie.

He wished he had a stomachache. What Adam had was worse. Somehow, he really had lost control of his life. This wasn't the fun kind of losing control, like careening down the Giant Chute at Splosh-Splosh Water & Adventure Park on Route 119 in Riverdale. This was scary—like being swept along the waters of the Tremble River in a raging flood.

His parents were still at work. He walked in and went up to his room, closed the door, and flopped onto his bed. He was going to sleep; that was his plan—be asleep when his mom and dad got home, so he didn't have to answer more questions.

But he could not make his brain stop. He just lay there.

Everyone—Devillio, the five vile predators, Mrs. Finch, Mrs. Quigley, Jennifer, Jennifer's mom, his parents, even that pip-squeak Phoebe—seemed to move quicker than he did these days, outmaneuvering him at every turn. His life had changed so fast. That black SUV (*Or was it midnight charcoal? This was the kind of question that filled Adam's mind now.*) was there one minute, gone the next. Yet in those sixty seconds, the car doors had been thrown open and inscrutable forces had been let loose. Adam had been converted from man of action to pathetic victim.

Why hadn't he punched that kid back?

He felt exhausted, but he'd even forgotten how to sleep.

While he was tossing and thrashing, trying to get comfortable, he noticed the books Jennifer had given him, scattered across his bedroom floor. He reached for the nearest one. On the back cover was a picture of that Erik Forrest guy in military fatigues and a flak jacket hopping off a helicopter in a ducked-down position.

Maybe reading about a war or two would take his mind off his own problems.

chapter 6

Exploding Pancakes

"You have to do this," said his dad. "Your friend Jennifer said she needs it for the front page. She called Mom three times."

They were driving to the mall bookstore, where Adam was supposed to have his exclusive interview with the world-famous war reporter, Erik Forrest. It was Adam's first time out in days, except for school. He'd barely left his room. He just stayed in bed reading anything close by. He read the books Jennifer had given him. He reread all his old *Mad* magazines and the Dr. Seuss and William Steig picture books he'd loved when he was little. He read every word of the operator's manuals for his CD player and for the outdoor Ping-Pong table. Anything not to think his own thoughts.

He didn't want to talk to anybody, let alone a great reporter who'd remind Adam of what a failure he was.

They'd stopped. His dad reached across Adam's lap and opened the door. "You'll be fine," his father said. "Two great reporters exchanging ideas. You'll have lots to talk about."

Adam trudged toward the bookstore.

"Adam!" his father called.

He felt a surge—maybe his dad changed his mind.

"You forgot this," he said, holding up the backpack with the Erik Forrest books.

When Adam reached the section of the bookstore for celebrity author appearances, he got a sick feeling. There was a TV crew, three radio reporters, a couple of people with laptops who seemed like they might be bloggers, and a reporter and photographer from the *Citizen-Gazette-Herald-Advertiser.* Some exclusive. Adam hated being lied to. Too bad Jennifer wasn't there; she could have reminded him why this was such a terrific story.

He pulled out his notebook and squeezed between a TV sound person and the photographer.

For a moment, Adam thought he was in the wrong place. The guy they were listening to didn't look like the man on the book cover hopping off the helicopter. He looked like somebody's grandfather.

Worse than that, Adam could not believe what he was hearing. The world-famous war reporter was talking about pancakes. He was talking about his book, *Someone Help Me: The Pancakes Are Exploding!* The cover blurb said it was supposed to be this hilarious account of a war correspondent trying to adjust to becoming a stay-at-home dad.

Of all the things Adam had read in his bedroom that week, *Pancakes Are Exploding!* was the most boring, worse than the operator's manual for the CD player.

Chapter after chapter described the world-famous reporter realizing how hard it was being a full-time housewife—getting to the bus stop late, spoiling the laundry by putting in a red tie-dyed shirt. Big deal. Adam's dad did that every day and his father had a job.

Adam was growing angrier by the minute. Now Mr. World-Famous was telling them the exact story that was in the book about trying to make pancakes for the first time and placing a pitcher on the hot stove by mistake and having it shatter, cutting World-Famous in three places.

"I was hurt worse making pancakes than in any war," he said, and all the press people howled and so did World-Famous, as if he hadn't told that story a hundred times.

"So, to be safe," said Peter Friendly, of Cable News 12, "get out of the kitchen and go to war!"

"Exactly," said World-Famous, laughing uproariously.

It got worse. A young man and woman from the publisher, with matching khaki pants and yellow button-down shirts, ushered them over to a fake cardboard kitchen display to take photos of Forrest in an apron and paper chef hat.

Nearby was a press table stocked by the publisher with fancy deli sandwiches, cookies, brownies, and bottled water. The news people were wolfing down free food.

Adam had never met any real writers and

assumed they'd have a wise aura around their heads. This guy was a clown.

In fact, the whole event felt like a circus. Adam had always believed that Jennifer's rule about not taking food or anything else from people you were writing about was too strict. But watching these press people—they seemed like pigs, filling bags with food to take home.

Adam couldn't wait for them to leave. Fortunately, one story seemed to be all they needed. The female assistant took Forrest's arm and started leading him out.

"Great sound bite," she said.

"I'm getting good at this," said Forrest.

"Excuse me," said Adam. "Hey, excuse me."

They stopped.

Adam told them his name and newspaper and explained that he had been promised an exclusive interview with Mr. Forrest.

"We just had that fabulous press opportunity," said the woman. "You could have asked any question."

"It's not the same. This says exclusive," said Adam, showing the e-mail Jennifer gave him.

The woman took it reluctantly. "Oh, this," she

said. "Actually it says *local* exclusive. That means, at your school, you're the only paper we invited."

"The *Slash* is the only paper at our school," said Adam. "That's exclusive nothing."

"Wait," said Mr. Forrest. "We promised this young man an exclusive?" The woman rolled her eyes, but she did nod; Adam saw it. "Then we will keep our promise." They were near the front of the store, and Forrest led Adam to two soft chairs in the literature section.

The woman reminded Forrest that they needed to leave in ten minutes for the next mall, then hurried off.

"It's Adam, right?" said Forrest. "How can I help you, Adam? You want a story I didn't tell the rest of the pack? Here's your exclusive. I was doing a wash—"

"I know," said Adam. "The red tie-dyed shirt. I read the book."

Forrest stared at Adam. "You read *Pancakes Are Exploding!*? My God. No one ever reads the book. What did you think?"

What did he think? The last time Adam spoke truth to power, he'd been flattened by Devillio. And this guy was Mr. World-Famous. Finally Adam said, "It wasn't that great."

"Fabulous," said Forrest. "The only reporter on the twelve-city tour who reads the book, and you hated it."

"It's not that I hated it," said Adam. "It's like, I didn't think it was worthy of you."

Forrest's face softened. "Ah," he said, "that is different."

"My coeditor, Jennifer, gave me a bunch of your books," Adam continued, "and the war ones — they were amazing. The way you were in the helicopter with that wounded Marine being airlifted out of the fighting. I mean, this was way before I was born, but when I read it, I felt like the soldier just died that second. It's like I miss him even though I never met him."

Adam's eyes had welled up and he was too embarrassed to look at Forrest. But then Forrest blew his nose and Adam noticed that Forrest's eyes looked moist, too.

"Jesus, Adam," said Forrest. "How did such a little boy get such an enormous heart? You know how I feel right now?" He got up, walked along the wall of literature, stopped at the *D*s, and returned with a book, which he held up for Adam. Charles Dickens's *A Christmas Carol.* "Seeing you," said Forrest, "so young and idealistic and hungry for truth — I feel like I'm Ebenezer Scrooge meeting the ghost of my past self. I'm looking at you, but I feel like I'm looking at the old me."

He sat down. "What do you want to ask, Adam? You've earned your exclusive."

Adam didn't know how to say it. He wanted to know how such a great reporter could wind up doing such an unimportant book. He wanted to know it as much for himself as for the story.

"Speak up," said Forrest. "Now's no time to get shy. The khaki-pantsers will be back any second. You've told me my book stinks. After that, any question should be easy."

Adam asked how a writer makes sure that he's doing stuff that matters and not compromising his principles. "It's not just you, Mr. Forrest — it's me, too," Adam said. "I feel like I've lost my confidence. Everything I do turns bad lately. I was so sure my investigative story on parents doing their kids' science projects was good but everyone thought I was a jerk. I feel . . . lost. I just want to feel like a great reporter again. How do you know if you're any good?"

"Ahhh," said Forrest. "Tough one. But I can tell you this. There were a dozen newspeople here today, and only one is willing to work hard enough to get it right. Only one is still asking questions. That's inside of you. It's your attitude, your energy, the standards you bring to the story."

Adam was taking notes.

"I don't meet many great reporters, even at the best papers and magazines. I meet lots of pretty good ones, but very few men and women willing to dig all the way down until they hit truth. Most just want enough facts to fill the space. Your question's a beaut, but it's not just your question. The very greatest have asked it, too." He stood up and walked along the bookshelf. "Stop me anywhere," he said.

"Now," said Adam. They were in the *F*s. Forrest pulled out two books by William Faulkner. "Nobel Prize–winning novelist," said Forrest. "Can't get any greater. Drank himself into a stupor trying to make easy money writing for movies."

Forrest was walking again.

"Now," Adam said.

They were at the *K*s and Forrest pulled out

The Castle by Franz Kafka. "You said you weren't sure about the science fair story? Kafka wasn't either. When he died, you know what his orders were? 'Burn all my books.' He thought they were trash. Thank God they didn't listen." Forrest motioned to the wall of books. "Smart people," he said. "And still, many got lost. What they thought was good was bad; what they thought was bad was good. But you can't stop trying."

"A question," said Adam. "You know that story about Kafka? Do you think when you die, you'll have them burn *Pancakes Are Exploding!*?"

Forrest leaned forward. "Between you and me? I'm going to burn it right after this interview."

"What I mean is, how could you?" asked Adam.

"Well, the short answer," said Forrest, "is I got lazy. The more famous I became, the less time I spent reporting and the more time I spent doing cable news shows — Erik Forrest, expert war correspondent."

"What's the long answer?" asked Adam.

"Ever been married, Adam?" asked Forrest.

"Um, no."

"Didn't think so," said Forrest. "Like somebody?"

"Not really," said Adam. "Well, sort of. A little bit."

"Well, I've liked too many somebodies. One day I'm having a drink at a party, and I mention I'm worried my third marriage is going down the toilet, so I'm trying to travel less and help out more around the house. And a sharp young book editor says, 'Erik Forrest's next war will be fought on the home front. Erik Forrest *is* Mr. Mom.' You know what that is, Adam?"

Adam didn't.

"High concept," said Forrest.

"What's that?" asked Adam.

"It's basically a book or movie where the only important part is the title," said Forrest. "You ask why I wrote it? I figured this was going to be the easiest two hundred thousand dollars I ever made."

"You got two hundred thousand dollars for *this?*" said Adam, wiggling *Pancakes Are Exploding!* at Forrest.

"Yes," said Forrest. "That was the advance. You putting that in your story?"

"Was it off the record?" asked Adam.

"Nah, you can use it," said Forrest. "Just do me a favor? Send me a copy of whatever you write? I'm dying to see what you make of all this.

"To answer your original question," Forrest

continued, "my prescription for being a great reporter is: First, always keep reporting until you get to the bottom of the story. Dig, dig, dig. Second, never forget that the people you're interviewing are the story, not you. Third, don't do cable news shows. And fourth, drink lots of fluids — nonalcoholic are best."

Adam loved tips. He could see running a sidebar with the main story headlined "Erik Forrest's Four Tips to Great Reporting."

The khaki-pantsers were ready to go, but Forrest gave them twenty dollars and told them to find a bar and have a few big pink drinks with fruit sticking out the top. "Just call the next mall and say, 'This Erik Forrest is a hothead and we're running late.' The public loves hothead writers. I promise, when we get there, I'll tell them all the stories they can stand — I'll even throw in the one about almost getting arrested for leaving the kids alone, double-parked in the van outside the bank."

"That one was actually pretty good," said Adam.

"Oh, met your standards, did it?" said Forrest. "I'm relieved."

Forrest used the time to ask Adam about the *Slash*. It was fun for Adam; Forrest really was a great reporter, and he got every story that Adam described right away. Adam mentioned the investigation that got Marris fired as principal; he shared his plan for the science fair story; he told Forrest how they had stopped the basketball hoops from being torn down by the Tremble Zoning Board chairwoman, Mrs. Boland.

"Mrs. Boland," repeated Forrest. "Any relation to Boland Cable?"

"The same," said Adam.

"Impressive," said Forrest. "Be careful. You upset powerful people like the Bolands, they can squeeze you hard. They don't forget." Forrest took out his wallet and gave Adam his card. "If I can ever help, you call," he said. "I mean it." He got up.

"Mr. Forrest," said Adam, "this was great. I learned so much. I'll never forget it."

"Thanks, Adam," said Forrest. "Me, too."

When Adam got home, he went to the computer for the first time in days and wrote to Jennifer. He was afraid he'd get her away message, but she was online.

I'M BACK! he wrote.

How'd it go? she wrote.

No, I mean I'M BACK!

I know, she wrote. *Was he good?*

You don't get it, he wrote. *I'M BACK! I feel like I've busted through a fog I've been stuck in ever since that stupid shoveling thing. I'M BACK!*

Ohhhhhhh. YOU'RE BACK! Thank heavens. I need you BACK!

She wrote that she'd gotten Phoebe's story on the three-hundred-year-old tree that the state wanted to cut down and it was awful. She said she'd e-mail him a copy.

Great! he wrote. *On the ride home, I figured out my science project. It'll make a great Spotlight investigation, too. The Devil's going down!*

What a day. He was ready for bed.

But before he put on his away message, Jennifer wrote again: *Sweet dreams. Am in my nighty saying nighty-nighty.*

Adam laughed out loud. Jennifer really could get a little fruity sometimes.

chapter 7

The Whole Truth

Adam had never felt so energetic, so focused. At the Quiz Bowl Gladiator meet, he banged his buzzer so fast, the opposing team sat paralyzed. The plumes on their gray plastic helmets drooped miserably.

At basketball practice, he was on fire. Coach had the first and second teams scrimmage. Adam was the point guard on the second team, and they usually lost to the starters. Today they demolished them. Adam hit twelve-footers, eighteen-footers, even a couple of threes. He crossed over the first team point guard, Tish Osborne, so bad that Tish fell, and Adam got to offer him a hand up—the ultimate insult.

"Floor's slippery," Tish mumbled. "No way you crossed me."

"I know," said Adam, smiling straight into his lying face.

At dinner they had the Chinese salad his dad was so proud of—cabbage, scallions, soy chicken, noodles, toasted almonds, a vinegar-and-oil dressing. Normally, Adam's response was, "Dad, can you heat up some frozen chicken nuggets? There's too much going on in this salad." Tonight he could have happily consumed another fifty ingredients.

Sleep problems? Ha! His head hit the pillow and he was out. Fast at Quiz Bowl, fast at basketball, and fast asleep.

Jennifer was surprised. Usually Adam sat alone at lunch or with a buddy. She liked that he wasn't attached to any group. But today he was with the basketball team—not the easiest collection of human beings.

The moment they saw her, they gave her a hard time. "Looking for your *Slash* bunny, honey?" one asked.

"Your hoop dream?" said another.

"No," said Tish Osborne, the best player and mouthiest. "Basketball's a little common for Jen. She's a tennis girl—thirty-love, right, cookie?"

"Shut up, Tish," said Jennifer, "or next time I see you on the court, I'll cross you so bad, the entire team won't be able to scrape you up."

Several boys went, "Ooooooooh," and Tish stood.

"Never been crossed and never will," he said. "You hear any different?"

"I do," said Jennifer. "I hear you been crossing every day to walk home on Ashley Wheatley's side of the street. I hear for some reason, Ashley Wheatley thinks you're cute."

There were "Oooooooohs" again, but Tish liked them this time and a bad moment passed.

Adam slid his leg over the bench seat and slipped away. "Got to go," he said. "Duty calls."

The two found a table on the edge of the lunchroom. "Since when are you a jock?" Jennifer asked.

"I play five sports," said Adam.

"Right," said Jennifer. "But there's a difference between playing sports and being a jock. You with the hot boys now?"

Adam smiled. "A few starters grabbed me and said, 'You play like the first team, you got to eat with the first team.'"

"Poor baby," she said. "You had no choice."

"Doesn't matter," he said. "You fixed that. Tish is going to wipe the floor with me at practice. How'd you know I crossed him?"

Jennifer loved that about Adam. All the low-life gossip and chitchat whizzed right by him. "It's all over school," she said. "I believe the correct term is 'broke his ankles'?"

"You're lucky to be a girl," said Adam. "If I said that stuff to Tish, he'd break every bone I own. But he won't go after you — *I'll* pay."

He had a point, but all Jennifer said was, "Maybe.

"That wasn't about you anyway," she went on. "I couldn't let Tish get away with that cookie crap. You know what that is, right?"

Adam nodded, though he didn't have a clue. He found it impossible to keep up with all the inside stuff.

"I just said what popped into my head," she said.

"Forget it," said Adam. "He'd be looking to get even anyway. I didn't realize — seems like you know him."

Jennifer nodded. "I've been in his class a lot," she said. "He's not mean like he seems sometimes. You should see him with his little brother, Tyrone. Calls him Ty-Ty. He can actually be very sweet."

Adam nodded. He just knew Tish from basketball and hadn't personally witnessed a lot of Tish's sweetness.

"It's hard to know people when everyone's so busy sticking it to everyone," said Jennifer. "You understand why they had you at their table? They were sticking it to Tish. They were using you to remind Tish that first string's on the line. You don't think they suddenly wanted to be your best friend?"

"For a minute I did," Adam said.

Jennifer gave him her super fisheye.

"Maybe not an entire minute."

"We've got problems," she said, going into her backpack and pulling out Phoebe's tree story. "What do I do with this?"

Adam's answer surprised her. He liked the story. He admitted it had a few weak spots, but he had gotten all excited when he realized that the three-hundred-year-old tree in question was the climbing tree. The state was talking about cutting down the

81

climbing tree! He loved that tree, and it sure didn't look like it was dying. The tree had a full crown of leaves in summer, and the trunk felt plenty hard last time Adam accidentally skidded his bike into it. After the big snow, he'd seen kids using it for cover in a snowball fight. A few had climbed into the lower branches and were dropping snow bombs.

For Adam, it was a tree impossible not to climb. The branches spread upward, like a ladder. Most kids were too scared to go for the high ones, but ever since he was little, Adam had been a great climber and actually reached the top once. He could see for miles.

At that moment, Jennifer had no patience for Adam's fond childhood memories. She'd expected a little coeditor unity.

"A few weak spots?" she said. "What about the lead-in describing Phoebe's 'emotion-laden' visit during 'what might be this magnificent specimen's final, tragic winter'? And her thoughts on how this relates to her recent appointment as third-grade recycling captain? And her twelve-line quote from Dr. Seuss about 'the Lorax, who speaks for the trees . . .'"

"'Who speaks for the birds, who speaks for the bees,'" recited Adam. It was his favorite Dr. Seuss.

Jennifer was glaring at him.

"Stay calm," Adam said. "You've got a point. You could probably cut out the first twenty-three graphs without hurting the story."

"And there's no one giving the state's side," said Jennifer. "The state must have some reason for wanting to cut it down. She makes it sound like tree murder."

"Right," said Adam. "Got to get a comment from the state. But—bad pun intended—you're missing the forest for the trees. This is a three-hundred-year-old tree, and though I can't exactly tell from Phoebe's story, here's my guess. There's one reason to cut it down and one reason not to and they're practically the same.

"On one hand, it's lived three hundred years, and could fall over tomorrow, crushing innocent people. On the other hand, it's lived for three hundred years and it hasn't crushed a soul, so why are they suddenly hot to cut it down? My reporter's instinct tells me something rotten's going on."

Jennifer was holding her head to stop it from exploding. "If you love it so much, you edit it."

"No thanks," said Adam. "Phoebe's your specialty. She thinks I don't like her, remember?"

"Could you at least come when I talk to her?"

Adam could. Basketball practice was late today.

Jennifer asked if he'd phoned the lady from the Willows, Mrs. Willard, about renaming that street for Dr. King.

"No," he said. "But I heard something at lunch."

"Tell me," she said.

"Wait," he said. "Weren't you the one making fun of me for having lunch with those guys? It's good for reporters to mix with different groups. You should try it."

"You are hilarious," she said. "Tell me."

"It wasn't so much what they were saying," Adam said. "More the attitude. Like naming the street for Dr. King was a joke. The other thing I couldn't follow exactly, but they were saying stuff about the Bolands."

"Who said?" asked Jennifer.

"Tish. Some of his friends."

"Tish lives in the Willows," said Jennifer.

Adam pulled out his To-Do list and circled Mrs. Willard's name for emphasis. His list was an all-time record, three feet eight inches long. When it hit forty-eight inches, it would be tall enough to ride the Giant Chute at Splosh-Splosh Water & Adventure Park on Route 119.

He had to finish his abstract for his new science fair project. He had a practice DBQ—data-based question—due for before-school/after-school voluntary/mandatory class for the state test. He had to call Outraged Single Mother.

He had to go to basketball and get wiped by Tish.

By the time they got to Room 306, Phoebe was waiting, fiddling with a camera. "Want to see the tree?" she asked. She'd gotten a digital camera for Christmas and used the screen to show them. Most photos were Phoebe standing in front of the tree. Phoebe had apparently taken the pictures herself, using the self-timing device, because in a few frames there was a blur that appeared to be Phoebe racing to get in the picture. And that wasn't the worst of it. The tree trunk was so wide—eight feet, according to the story—and the photos were shot so close up, the pictures looked like Phoebe standing in front of a wall.

"You can't tell it's a tree," said Jennifer.

"I know," said Phoebe. "If I stood far enough back to get most of the tree in, I was just a dot. So I compromised. I figured people would be able to tell from the headline that it was a tree.

"So you liked the story?" asked Phoebe.

Jennifer said, "There's a lot of good stuff in there."

For a moment, Phoebe's eyes got huge, then, while still sitting straight in her chair, she flopped her head back until she was staring at the ceiling. "You hated it," she moaned.

"No," said Jennifer.

"Yes," said Phoebe, still staring at the ceiling. "Everyone knows that if editors say something's perfect, then you have to change maybe a third of it. And if they say it's a couple of small things, that's about half. And if they say there's a lot of good stuff in there—well, you might as well just throw the whole story away and shoot yourself."

"You're overreacting," said Jennifer. "It's going to be great. But the story's like the photos—too much you. Not enough tree."

"You don't like the start?" said Phoebe, lifting her head to look at Jennifer, then flopping it back. "That's where all the feeling is."

Jennifer said feeling was good, but twenty-three paragraphs was too much.

"Too much?" said Phoebe. "I already cut it way back. It used to be forty-two graphs."

Jennifer said they needed to talk to state officials and that might give them an idea about how to redo the story. "We'll figure this out," said Jennifer. "Just stop looking at the ceiling."

"I did bad," said Phoebe.

"All reporters, no matter how great, have stories that give them trouble," said Jennifer. "Adam came totally unglued during his science fair investigation."

"Really?" said Phoebe, looking over at Adam. "You?"

"Not totally," said Adam. "I was still able to walk and take nourishment."

Phoebe cheered up. Her head was still flopped back, but at least she was making sideways eye contact.

"Sometimes, when it comes to writing, less can be more," said Jennifer. She told Phoebe about *Night*, a book on the middle-school summer reading list. It was about the concentration camps in Germany during World War II. Practically every Harris middle-schooler chooses it because *Night* is the shortest book on the list at one hundred and twenty pages.

"Adam read the whole thing the last day of vacation," said Jennifer. "But then it turns out to be this moving story about a Jewish boy living in a death camp." Their English teacher said that the author, Elie Wiesel, was himself a death-camp survivor. And people always asked how after going through so much, did Wiesel write such a skinny book?

"You know his answer?" asked Jennifer.

"I totally give," said Phoebe.

"For every word in that book, there were ten that he cut," she said. "By cutting and making sure he chose the right word, he turned an eight-hundred-and-sixty-four-page first draft into a one-hundred-twenty-page book. That's what they mean when they say less is more. So how about if you stop looking at the ceiling and we'll figure out the best way to redo this."

"That's a pretty good story," said Phoebe. "Only one thing. If less is more, how come the fourth Harry Potter is seven hundred thirty-four pages?"

"What?" said Jennifer.

"And the fifth is eight hundred seventy pages."

"She has a point," said Adam.

"Shut up!" shouted Jennifer. "Phoebe, you unflop your head right now and sit up. We're going to edit this story, and it's going to come in at somewhere under eight hundred seventy pages!"

"Geez," said Phoebe, straightening up at long last. "No need to get worked up. You sound like *him*."

"She does, doesn't she?" said Adam. "Jennifer, you have to work on controlling your outbursts."

"Right," said Jennifer. "Phoebe, pull out your notes. Maybe that'll help me figure this out."

Phoebe produced a folder, which Jennifer pored through, asking several questions.

"Ahhh," Jennifer finally said. "I think I get it. The state has been sued a bunch of times because old trees keep falling on people. And these lawsuits blame the state for not keeping a close eye on dangerous trees. And when these people sue, they can get lots of money from the state. So to save money, the state decided to cut down old trees before they fall on anybody. And they're going to hold a hearing in March to let people know."

"I think that's it," said Phoebe.

"Then why didn't you put the state's reason in?" asked Jennifer. "There's nothing about dangerous trees falling on people."

Phoebe flopped her head back again, but Jennifer jumped up, grabbed Phoebe's head, and set it straight.

"No way," said Jennifer. "We're done flopping. Why isn't it in the story?"

With their faces so close, the tear rolling down Phoebe's cheek looked huge. "Oh geez, Phoebe, forget it," said Jennifer. "No big deal."

Adam handed Phoebe a tissue.

"I bet you were afraid if you put the state's reason in," Adam said, "it would be bad for the tree."

Phoebe nodded through her sniffles.

"I love that tree, too," Adam said.

chapter 8

Trouble, Trouble Everywhere . . .

Adam spent the evening making calls to people on his To-Do list. His goal was to get the list down to two feet.

Right away, he knew he'd dialed the right number for Mrs. Willard, the lady from the Willows, because from the first hello, she was yelling.

"My name's on that federal No Call list!" she hollered. "No way you sales vultures can call me." And she slammed down the phone.

Adam pressed redial.

"You again," she yelled. "I'm going to star-sixty-nine you so fast, your head'll spin. Consider yourself reported to the proper authorities. Hope you're set for a ten-thousand-dollar fine—and that's just first offenders, which I'm sure is not you."

"Mrs. Willard," Adam pleaded, "stop. It's me, Adam. Adam Canfield of the *Slash*. Remember? You helped me on the story about Miss Bloch leaving her money to Harris."

The line was quiet. She must have been debating whether to star-69 him. Finally she said, "How I know it's you?"

"If it wasn't me," said Adam, "would I know you make really good cocoa with little bobbing marshmallows?"

"That is me," she said. "So this must be you. How you doing, Adam?"

They had a nice time catching up. Mrs. Willard apologized for not calling after his story came out to say how much she'd enjoyed it—especially the part about her being a superb neighbor. And Adam apologized for not stopping by, like he'd promised.

Then he explained that they were trying to do a story on renaming the street in the Willows for Dr. King. He told her how the school had big plans for a celebration but no date yet. He said they didn't know exactly what was going on but smelled a rat.

"Bless your little white nose," said Mrs. Willard. "Ain't a thing wrong with your olfactory sense, child. A rat it is."

Adam was excited and asked if it was OK to take notes.

"Oh no," said Mrs. Willard. "You going to put me in every article you write? I'm not looking to be a regular feature in that *Slash*." She said he needed to speak to their minister at the Pine Street AME Zion Church. She said this was too touchy for someone like her, with loose lips and a waggy tongue. She suggested that Adam come by on Sunday, around three. The church mothers were holding their winter buffet. "Good eatin'," said Mrs. Willard.

"Oh, it won't be me," said Adam, explaining that Jennifer was doing the story.

"Wait," said Mrs. Willard. "I been expecting you. I know I can trust you. I seen you doing your reportering live-at-five. This story is easy to take the wrong way. I don't know no Jennifer."

"She's great," said Adam. "She was the byline with me on the Miss Bloch story. She's my coeditor. Actually, I'm her coeditor. She's a better editor than me. The whole paper would collapse without Jennifer."

"That so?" said Mrs. Willard. "You sweet on that girl?"

"Nah," said Adam.

"That so?" said Mrs. Willard. "Guess I got that wrong. Please accept my apologies. I was hallucinating. Now I sure hope I can trust you, child. This so-called friend Jennifer — she going to be comfortable in a church full of black folk?"

"I think so," said Adam. "Jennifer's black."

"That so?" said Mrs. Willard. "Whose girl is she? She's not in the Willows?"

Adam told Mrs. Willard about Jennifer's parents, her mom being a PTA honcho, her dad a lawyer in the city, her third-grade twin sisters, their dog SayHey, their house in River Bluffs.

"River Bluffs," repeated Mrs. Willard. "Sounds like you got yourself one of them rich Jennifers."

"Jennifer's not like that," said Adam. "She's not snotty, Mrs. Willard. She's pretty normal. Honest."

"Uh-huh," said Mrs. Willard. "OK. I guess that'll have to do. Reverend Shorty's a big man; he can take care of himself. We going to find out exactly how normal your Jennifer is."

Adam thanked her and crossed her off his To-Do list. But Mrs. Willard wasn't done. "While I got you," she said, "there's a bigger story here in the Willows. I tried to tell you last time you was here. You know how Minnie's house was boarded up—"

"Mrs. Willard," said Adam. "Can I ask a favor? Would you mind telling Jennifer? My To-Do list—it's almost four feet long."

"All righty," said Mrs. Willard. "Forget it. You got what you wanted. You got to be going now." And she hung up.

Adam called his grown-up friend Danny several times, but kept getting the answering machine. He needed to talk to someone about the shoveling case and knew Danny would be honest with him. His parents were being so nice, it was wearing him out. They kept asking how he was feeling. "You OK, Adam?" "Anything you want to discuss, Adam?" They were overjoyed that he'd come out of his room, but it was like they were checking to see if he'd crack up again. He didn't know how to answer them. And their nervousness made him nervous that he wasn't nervous enough.

Adam wanted to know if Danny thought he'd have to testify in court. What would happen when

Adam said he'd seen only two kids' faces? Should he pretend he saw them all? He didn't even know who grabbed him from behind.

Adam sent Danny e-mails but got no response, which was strange. When Danny was worked up, he could shoot Adam ten e-mails an hour.

Where was Danny?

And Danny wasn't the only one missing. Adam had no luck reaching Outraged Single Mother for his science fair investigation and after leaving several messages, crossed her off his list.

It was an amazing weekend, the kind that comes once a winter. After two months of temperatures ranging from single digits to the thirties, a warm front sneaked in from the south. It was in the high fifties and felt warmer. Adam couldn't figure it out. In summer, if the temperature dropped to the fifties, he was freezing and needed a heavy sweatshirt. But in winter, if it went up to the fifties, a T-shirt and sports shorts were plenty. He'd once asked Danny, who explained that Adam had pinpointed a classic example of Bernoulli's inverse windchill phenomenon.

However, Adam was never sure if it was that or if he'd pinpointed a case of Danny teasing him.

Whichever, the soft breeze off the river made Adam hungry to play ball at the Rec courts. Those courts were the center of basketball in Adam's part of Tremble. There were six outdoor hoops and lights for night play. Even grown-ups came around for games.

The bad news was that Adam had swim practice. The good news was that the pool was near the courts. So, along with his swim things, Adam took a bag with a basketball and money for food. Danny had once said that a basketball and a few dollars were all a kid needed for a happy life, and Adam agreed.

The courts looked great. The snow had melted, and someone was out early to squeegee away the puddles. For a long time, Adam shot alone. When he got warm, he took off his sweatshirt and sweatpants. As more kids showed and the courts filled, boys asked to shoot with him. He played several two-on-two and three-on-three half-court games. They always chose his ball. It was a good feeling, having a ball older kids respected.

By late morning, most of the first stringers from the Harris team showed up, including Tish. They nodded from a distance. Tish wasn't angry anymore; he'd wiped Adam all over the court the last two practices.

They were choosing teams for a full-court game—a lot of ninth and tenth graders, maybe two-thirds of them black. Tish was picked early. When each team needed one more, Tish leaned his head toward the tenth grader making the picks, who pointed at Adam and said, "Him."

Taking advantage of Bernoulli's inverse wind-chill, they played skins and shirts. Adam was relieved to be a shirt; his body was pretty skinny. He hit one outside shot, but that was all he took. They didn't know him, rarely passed to him. Mostly he touched the ball when he stole it or a rebound bounced his way. Then he'd dish off quick, usually to Tish.

As morning passed into afternoon, more older kids came. Some were high-school players, some out of high school. The next full-court game, Tish was the only middle-schooler picked.

Adam was ready to go, but they were using his

ball. He'd waited too long to say something. He decided to hang around until the game ended and plopped down on the sideline, his back against the chain-link fence.

From his bag, he pulled out a can of iced tea and drained it. He was starving and considered going back to the Rec pool and getting something from the vending machines, but figured he'd better stay and watch his ball.

"Noticing anything about how the courts are nice and dry?"

Adam startled. What jerk was talking in his ear?

He turned from the game to look over his shoulder. Someone was crouching on the other side of the fence, his head inches from Adam's. Adam was about to make a comment, then realized who it was.

"Hey, Shadow," said Adam. "How's it going?"

"I don't know," said the other boy. "How's it going?"

"Great," said Adam. "Couldn't be better." As Adam stood to talk more easily, the other boy stood too, his timing in sync with Adam's. He moved like Adam's reflection.

Shadow's face was pressed against the chain links, and Adam backed up a step so their noses wouldn't bump. The boy was wearing a bubble jacket that was too big zipped to his chin, and his fingers were hidden in the jacket's arms. An orange wool cap covered his ears.

"Aren't you warm?" asked Adam. "It's like spring."

"It is not like spring," said Shadow. "Spring begins March twentieth." He pushed up his sleeve and looked at his watch. "Today is January thirtieth, 1:23 P.M. Definitely winter."

"You're a hard man to argue with," said Adam.

"I am a hard man to argue with," said Shadow. "Why is that?"

"You just know a lot of stuff," said Adam.

Shadow nodded. "I do," said Shadow. "Not every watch has the date. Want to see?" He held it against the fence for Adam, then looked at it again himself. "It's the numbers in the little square. Still January thirtieth," said Shadow. "Except 1:24 P.M. One minute since I checked."

Adam nodded. Shadow was definitely not the easiest person to talk to. He was at Harris Middle, too, but was in special ed, the famous Room 107A. A few geniuses actually called him "107A," though mostly he was Shadow. The boy had this uncanny ability to suddenly materialize and, if he liked you, follow you around asking questions. Adam occasionally noticed him around town at odd hours—early Saturday morning, when Adam was going to swim practice, or weekday nights, if Adam had a baseball game under the lights.

Always alone.

Adam had been in his class one year in the early grades. His real name was Theodore. Adam couldn't remember his other name and didn't see him much now. Since middle school, Adam had been in honors classes and Shadow wasn't in any of those.

It was easy to tell there was something off about Shadow; his questions could get really annoying. But the stuff he said was surprising, too. He had such a fresh take on things—it made Adam smile inside. Shadow wasn't stupid; it was more complicated than that, but he sure didn't say stuff the regular way.

"It's not polite not to answer a person's question," said Shadow. "You know that."

"Uh-oh," said Adam. "Did I not answer a question?"

"You did not answer a question," said Shadow. "Do you want to know the question?" Adam nodded.

"The question was, 'Noticing anything about how the courts are nice and dry?'"

"Oh, right," said Adam. "They are nice and dry."

"I guess you want to know who made them nice and dry," said Shadow.

It was Shadow, of course. He told Adam that he had a job working as a special assistant to Mr. Johnny Stack, supervisor for the Tremble Recreation Department. Shadow described how he'd broomed and squeegeed the court—puddle by puddle—plus all the other things he did for his job, like picking up trash, putting up the goalie nets on the roller rink, and painting the benches at the tennis courts. "I make four dollars an hour, cash on the barrel," said Shadow. "Mr. Johnny Stack pays me off the books, so don't worry about it. Mr. Johnny Stack says, best not to tell too many people. Why did I tell you?"

"It's OK," said Adam. "I'll keep it secret."

"Just telling one person," said Shadow, "is not telling too many people."

Adam glanced over his shoulder. Was this game ever going to end?

"Want to see my Roger Clemens rookie card?" Shadow said. He took his wallet from his back pocket and pulled out the card, which was framed in clear plastic. "No one can touch it except me," he said. "Nearly mint condition."

The game was winding down, finally. Adam wanted to get going and said so to Shadow. Most kids would have understood, but Shadow wasn't great at taking hints.

"I know something about you that you don't know about me," said Shadow.

"I give," said Adam.

"It's not polite to give up too fast," said Shadow. "You have to say an answer."

Adam tried to think of something. "You can touch your tongue to your nose and I can't," he said.

"Can I do that?" said Shadow, sticking out his tongue but not reaching his nose. "I didn't know if I could. But I can't."

"Can I give up?" asked Adam.

"Yes," said Shadow. "The thing I know about you that you don't know about me is my brother's been arrested—"

"Wow, you know lots of stuff," said Adam, who was watching the game again. Adam was remembering how you could give Shadow pat answers to keep the conversation moving without draining your brain.

"Next basket wins!" a kid hollered. Adam needed

to slip in and get his ball. He needed something to eat, too — he was starved.

"He's going to jail," said Shadow. "Guess who—"

Adam felt bad ignoring Shadow, but he just wanted to go home. His patience was about over. "I give," said Adam.

"It's not polite to give too fast," said Shadow. "You have to answer. Mr. Johnny Stack says conversation is a two-way street."

Adam did not have a clue what they were talking about. "Hot fudge sundae," said Adam, who was wishing for one right now.

"That does not count," said Shadow. "You're supposed to guess a person who's making my brother—"

"What person?" said Adam, who was completely lost.

A heavy kid banked in a shot and someone shouted, "Game!" Kids were giving each other fives and knucks.

"Guess who is making my brother go to jail," said Shadow.

Adam hurried onto the court. A tall kid had his ball. The boy was moving off the court, dribbling and talking to a friend. Adam just wanted to grab his ball and go.

"You have to answer," called Shadow. "It's not polite."

Adam trotted up to the tall kid. "Need my ball," Adam said, trying to sound casual. "Got to go."

The tall boy stopped and looked at Adam like Adam was garbage. "I don't know nothing about this being your ball," the tall boy said. "I don't see no name, and I sure don't see your fingerprints. Be getting home, junior cheese; you don't want to be starting."

"You have to answer!" Shadow yelled, his face pressed against the fence.

Adam repeated that it was his, but his voice was trembly, and when he tried to grab the ball, the tall boy dribbled behind his back and his laugh crackled in Adam's ears.

Adam could feel tears coming, the last thing he needed, and was about to lunge for the ball, when there was another voice, low and calm.

"Hey, Dex. Everything OK?"

The tall boy stopped his dribble, held the ball for a moment, then softly tossed it to Adam.

"My bad, junior cheese," the tall boy said.

Adam clutched the ball. Getting it back felt like a miracle.

Something suddenly dawned on him: *Guess who is making my brother go to jail?* How could Adam be such an idiot? He turned and scanned the sidelines, but there was just space between the chain links.

Adam wheeled back around. He needed to thank Tish; he owed him two thank-yous now. Jennifer had been right about him. But Tish was gone, too—not totally gone, but two courts over, shooting with older kids, including that boy Dex, their backs to Adam.

A single thought pounded in Adam's brain: I want to go home.

chapter 9

Going to Church

"Whoa, babies! Passing on the left!"

A bike zipped by and Jennifer startled, nearly losing balance. "Watch it!" she yelled. "What kind of idiot . . . ? Wait! I know exactly what kind." She hopped back on and caught up to him. "What are you doing here?"

"I missed you."

Jennifer rolled her eyes. "Right," she said.

"I thought maybe you could use some help," said Adam. They were a block from the Pine Street AME Zion Church in the Willows, where Jennifer was heading to interview Reverend Shorty about renaming the street for Dr. King.

Jennifer looked upset.

"What?" said Adam. "Can't a coeditor help a coeditor?"

"Look, I'm glad to see you," said Jennifer. "It's just—to get you rolling on a story, I usually have to chase you to the far corners of the earth, then pester you till the end of time. Now you suddenly drop out of the sky—it's weird. You think I can't do this story?"

"Of course you can," said Adam.

"You better not think I can't," she said. Jennifer was steamed. Before she had headed out that afternoon, even her father had tried giving her a big lecture on how Pine Street Church in the Willows was different from where they went. "Yes, I live in River Bluffs, and yes, I go to church at Saint Mark's Episcopal in North Tremble, but that doesn't mean I can't handle business in the Willows—"

"I know," said Adam. "That's exactly what I told Mrs. Willard."

"Told Mrs. Willard?" said Jennifer. "See! She *is* thinking that. It's the same thing as Tish giving me that cookie crap."

"What was that?" asked Adam. "I didn't get that."

"Oreo," said Jennifer. "Adam don't you know anything? Black on the outside, white on the inside. It's an insult for black people, like you forgot your roots."

"Jennifer," said Adam. "To me, you look like a Mrs. Radin's Famous Homemade Super-Chunk Buckets O' Chocolate Moisty Deluxe chocolate-chip cookie."

"What's that supposed to mean?" snapped Jennifer. "Is that racial, too?"

"No," said Adam. "It's my favorite cookie."

She was quiet. Then she gave him a smile — Adam hadn't seen many smiles like that. It made him feel all butterscotchy inside.

"Oh, Adam," she said.

"They're really delicious," he said.

"I guess so," she said. "So why *are* you here?"

"To be honest," said Adam, "I had a bad day yesterday. I don't want to stop . . . you know . . . being *back*. I mean, I'm *back*. I just want to stay back."

"Of course you're back," said Jennifer. "You are back."

"I thought a juicy investigation like this Dr. King

story would be good for me," he said. "Because, you know, I'm back."

"You're definitely back," said Jennifer. "Let's go. If *I* don't get back before dark, I'm dead."

As they locked their bikes to a No Parking sign out front, Jennifer said, "It is a big difference." Jennifer's church, Saint Mark's, was a towering stone structure, with large stained-glass windows, vaulted ceilings, and polished oak pews. Pine Street looked like a yellow ranch house with aluminum siding.

In the churchyard, little boys in white shirts and gray slacks and little girls in dresses and buckle shoes, their winter coats wide open, were racing around, shouting and playing.

On the way up the front walk, Adam thought he noticed Tish Osborne on the far side of the playground, watching over a bunch of squirrelly little boys. Adam started walking toward the boys, but Jennifer stopped him.

"Not now," she said. "We need to do this. I'm nervous to get started."

A woman led them to an office in the rear of the church, where Reverend Shorty and Mrs. Willard were talking.

"Well, hello," said Mrs. Willard. "If it isn't Ebony and Ivory, together in two-part harmony. How you doing, Adam? I haven't been expecting you."

"Hi, Mrs. Willard," said Adam. "Yeah. Well, I was feeling kind of guilty after our last phone call—"

"Good," said Mrs. Willard. "That was the idea. Sooo"—she was giving Jennifer a good up and down—"this is the famous Jennifer. Praise Jesus, Adam; you never cease to amaze me, boy. You got a sharp eye for a yummy-looking treat."

Adam had warned Jennifer, but she still looked mortified.

"Am I embarrassing you, child?" said Mrs. Willard.

"A little bit," said Jennifer, trying to sound diplomatic about being a yummy treat for the second time that day.

"Good," said Mrs. Willard. "I'm famous for it— ain't that so, Shorty? Oh, Lordy, what is wrong with me? I didn't introduce nobody. This here's our minister, Mr. Cyrus Williams, but when he's churching, he goes by Reverend Shorty. You'll never meet a finer man."

Reverend Shorty wasn't short. To Adam, the minister looked big enough to play power forward in the NBA. When they shook hello, their hands looked like kitten paws in Reverend Shorty's.

"Don't let Mrs. Willard here rattle you," Reverend Shorty said to Jennifer. "She is nowhere near as nasty as she'd like you to believe."

"One man's opinion," said Mrs. Willard.

Jennifer explained that the *Slash* editors suspected there was some problem with naming the street for Dr. King. "A source tipped off my coeditor here that people in the Willows are opposed to it," Jennifer said.

"That weren't no source," Mrs. Willard butted in again. "That was me. Hello."

"Um, Mrs. Willard," said Adam. "Remember you told me you didn't want to be in the paper? So I told Jennifer it was off the record."

"To protect you," said Jennifer.

"The boy was protecting me?" said Mrs. Willard. "You something, Adam. Can I ask a question? Now, Adam, you just close your ears. I want to ask Jennifer here something, folk to folk.

"First time I met your Adam," Mrs. Willard said, "he just rode his bike up Grand and started going about his reportering business like he was right at home. A lot of white boys, I don't think they'd be so comfortable. It's like he don't see color so much—you know what I'm saying?"

Jennifer did, though she'd never said it out loud before. She would have preferred keeping it a private thought, especially with Adam sitting there, but this lady had a major case of nose trouble.

"It's not so much that Adam's not prejudiced," Jennifer began. "It's more that he's totally oblivious. A lot of times, he's in a fog, and when he is paying attention, he only seems to notice big stuff."

"Geez," said Adam. "Is that a compliment or an insult?"

"Shush," said Mrs. Willard. "Your ears supposed to be closed."

"Well, it makes you rare," said Reverend Shorty. "We certainly could use a little more good oblivion in the world."

And Mrs. Willard said, "Amen to that, Shorty."

Jennifer had taken five pages of notes, but wasn't getting a thing. Every quote sounded dodgy. They asked if Reverend Shorty was upset about naming a street for Dr. King, and he talked about how much he admired Dr. King. They asked if he knew why there was no date for the ceremony, and he said that was a question to ask school and county officials. They asked if the minister had plans to lead a protest, and he said that plans were a dime a dozen but nothing was settled.

It frustrated the coeditors. What was wrong?

"This isn't doing you much good, is it?" Reverend Shorty said. "Can I make a suggestion? Put those pens down. . . . Now let's just talk, then we'll try to figure out if any of this can go in your paper."

Jennifer and Adam glanced at each other. They needed Reverend Shorty to tell the truth but feared they'd lose his great quotes. Even if he did agree to let them write the story when he finished, Reverend Shorty's quotes would be so guarded by then, they'd sound fake.

"How about this?" said Adam. "This is off the record; we can't use any of it unless you say. But we'd still like to take notes to remember the details—in case you do let us quote you."

"No," said Reverend Shorty. "This is too hot. It's not that we don't trust you—well, it is a little bit that—but mostly we need to go slow. This reaches to the top of Tremble County. If it comes out wrong, the Willows could be flattened. Literally."

"But—" said Jennifer.

"You listen," said Reverend Shorty, and his voice was stern. "There are people in this church who think I'm crazy talking to two kid reporters for a student paper. 'If that was some real newspaper, it wouldn't have no name like *Slash.*' That's what they say. But I prayed on it and decided there was two reasons to put my trust in you. Number one, no one else gives a bird turd about us. The *Citizen-Gazette-Herald-Advertiser* and News 12 would never do a story. They're owned by the Bolands. They print what the Bolands let them print, and the Bolands sure as hell aren't going to let this story out unless it's some puff job on all the great food the Boland Foundation is donating. So, you are all we have."

Adam felt like a pathetic last resort. Reverend Shorty was starting to seem mean.

"The second reason," he continued, "is that Mrs. Willard here says your paper did remarkable on the story about the crooked Harris principal. Says you appear to be truth tellers, which is a big compliment in our church. She thinks we can trust you. And Mrs. Willard—she's famous for having high standards."

Mrs. Willard was shaking her head. "You know, Rev," she said, "I put in a lot of time and effort, building a reputation as a foul-mouthed idiot. Now you go sugarcoating me."

"One man's opinion," Reverend Shorty said, smiling.

"Strictly off the record, these folks making all this hoopla about renaming that street don't have a clue what Dr. King stood for," Reverend Shorty said. "Church members, like Mother Willard—you know why she lives in the Willows? For years, she couldn't buy in no neighborhood except the Willows. None of our people could. I know men and women, hard-working Christians, they'd see a house for sale in some nice section of Tremble. They'd call; some even put on a white voice, fool those salespeople. But the moment our people arrived, their dark skin disqualified them. Suddenly the seller decides to take the house off the market or raise the price way up. Nothing you could prove—no, sir. Catching a man in the act of prejudice is as wispy as catching fog. It's all around; you feel it on your skin, smell it in your nostrils, see it plain as day, but you can't grab it and it's nothing you can carry into court."

"Now, Dr. King," Reverend Shorty went on, "he didn't stand for black people living with black and whites with white. King was an integration man."

"Hold on," said Mrs. Willard. "I didn't care nothing about living with whites. But I knew if I had a house on a street where whites would buy, I could sell my house for more money 'cause whites had more money.

"You look at the streets in this country named for Dr. King," Mrs. Willard continued. "Most cities, it's the worst streets — drug dealers on the corner. That ain't no way to honor Dr. King. You're reporters — go do some reportering. No one in the Willows signed no petition to have no street name switched." And here, Mrs. Willard made a disgusted, spitting noise. "You, girl, you live in River Bluffs. I bet it's nice. Maybe we should rename your street. You think white people on your street be dancing the jig if one morning they wake up and they're living on Martin Luther King Drive?"

Jennifer looked too shocked to say a word.

Reverend Shorty was out of his seat again, but

117

this time he stood behind Mrs. Willard and placed one large hand on each of her shoulders.

"Look at me, honey," he said to Jennifer. "You got no reason to feel bad. I've learned enough from Mother Willard here to fill a hundred books, but that don't mean we agree on everything. Maybe because I'm younger than Mother Willard, I'm more hopeful. . . ."

"Or more stupid," said Mrs. Willard, but she was laughing now.

"In my humble opinion, we are making progress," continued Reverend Shorty. "My grandpa was a stable man on an old Tremble River summer estate, and Daddy was a painter at the boatyard and here I am, second-shift foreman. And we got families coming to Tremble, like your daddy, got jobs at big city law firms. Don't look surprised, I know. Our people, they have professor jobs now, and doctor jobs. They can buy in River Bluffs or River Path or Riverdale or River View. And that's a proud thing, so long as you know where the story begins."

"We're not picking on you, girl," Mrs. Willard said, then jabbed her finger at Adam. "You think that nice little white coeditor—his folks going to move to Martin Luther King Drive? I'm talking to you, Mr. Ivory."

Adam couldn't think what to say, but Reverend Shorty saved him.

"Maybe Adam's parents would," Reverend Shorty said. "They've done a nice job so far. Now, we're only half done. We need to take a ride. To really see why our people's so outraged about the Bolands' jolly Dr. King party, you got to come along for Reverend Shorty's guided tour of the Willows, see what's going down."

"Um, Reverend Shorty, sir," said Adam. "One question. If you do the protest march, will that be at the renaming ceremony?"

"Don't think we'll have to," said Reverend Shorty.

"What?" said Jennifer.

"You'll figure it out," said Reverend Shorty, making it sound like a riddle with a trick answer. "Come on," he said, heading for the door. "If you need to be home before dark, we got to go." Then he loaded their bikes into the back of his pickup and drove Adam and Jennifer up and down the streets of the Willows, stopping at nine boarded-up houses, all with signs saying they'd been sold to Boland Realtors, Inc.

chapter 10

Theodore

It wasn't fair. Every time Adam crossed something off his To-Do list, something new popped on. He felt like he was in a Greek myth in Mr. Brooks's world history class, where the brave warrior Adameus chopped off the serpent's head, only to have two new to-dos grow back.

To do: His science fair abstract had to be in tomorrow.

To do: He needed to track down Shadow. The stuff Shadow had been saying that day at the courts—it must have had something to do with the mugging.

To do: He had to save the three-hundred-year-old tree story. Jennifer wanted to kill it! She didn't trust Phoebe's reporting, claimed Phoebe was biased in favor of the tree. Clearly, Jennifer had been exposed to a near-fatal overdose of Phoebe, and it had totally clouded her coediting judgment. Adam thought of Phoebe like radiation. She was great in small doses; she was a force for good when pointed at the right spot. But a sustained dose of Phoebe over a large area? It could destroy all mankind. He had to find some way to make Jennifer love that climbing tree as much as he and Phoebe did.

To do: They had to figure how to get the Dr. King story on the record.

To do: The deadline for the February *Slash* was just ten days away.

And Adam wasn't even counting stuff that he didn't *have* to do but wanted to do. Like see Danny.

Adam kept sending Danny e-mails, but hadn't heard back. That had never happened before. Danny was always there when Adam needed him. Where was Danny?

Adam knew he should ask his dad. His dad and Danny had been friends since college. His dad might know how Danny could disappear like this. Danny was a pretty exciting guy—he probably had some secret grown-up hideouts Adam didn't know. The problem was, Adam did not want his parents finding out why he was looking for Danny. Their latest thing was that he needed to talk to a quote-unquote "professional" about how the snow-shoveling mugging had traumatized him. Adam was really starting to get pissed off about it. Those five jerks who'd stolen his money were the psychos, not him.

Adam was ready to talk, but not with some "professional"—whatever that meant. He wanted Danny.

It was nearly midnight, and Adam was still staring at the science project title he'd written on his screen. The words had to be exactly right. In the last four months, he'd handed in four drafts for four different ideas, none of which he was actually going to do. Now he finally had a project he was excited about, but he needed to keep it secret for as long as possible.

If Adam didn't get the title perfect, he'd ruin everything. His title had to fake out Devillio. If he pulled it off, the whole science fair as it now worked—with parents doing the top projects—would come crumbling down. And in its place, Adam envisioned a *fair* fair.

Or something like that.

The problem was, if Devillio figured out too soon what Adam was up to, he would erupt worse than a papier-mâché volcano doused in Heinz vinegar. He'd kill Adam's idea; then he'd kill Adam.

Adam considered handing in a phony description and then secretly doing the real project. It might work. Devillio was famous for not reading his students' research papers. He was famous for not paying attention to anything, until the awards ceremony at the end of the fair, when the winners were announced. Adam was sure his secret project could win a top award before Devillio ever realized what was up. Adam would be onstage getting his prize, the packed auditorium cheering wildly, and it would be too late for the Devil to stop him.

There was only one problem. Devillio was famous for saving every scrap of paper, locked in dozens of filing cabinets in the stockroom next to his office. He kept copies of all the judging forms. He had science project papers he'd shown Adam's class that were twenty years old.

Adam worried that if he handed in a phony project description, Devillio would pull it out of his stupid stockroom files later on and use it to disqualify Adam. The Devil would make up a rule like "Any project that doesn't match its abstract is an automatic zero."

So Adam was gambling. He'd make his abstract basically truthful—*basically*. But he would also make the description so vague that it would be hard to tell what the project was really about.

He was hoping that Devillio would never read the abstract.

Or if Devillio did take a glance, Adam was hoping he'd only look at the title.

Or if by some miracle Devillio did read past the cover, Adam was betting that he'd only skim the first page.

For this reason, Adam had selected the largest font that he could get away with, 18 point, so there'd be as few words as possible on the first page. At the top, he put a quote from Emerson that sounded smart but said nothing: "Men love to wonder and that is the seed of science."

He worked hard so that you had to read to the end of the final page to have a clue what he was up to. And even then, you wouldn't be sure unless you knew what the project was.

For half an hour, he'd been staring at his latest title:

A SURVEY OF THE RELATIONSHIP BETWEEN
PARENT SUPPORT AND STUDENT SCORES

It was close, but not right. He stood up, walked around, jumped up and touched the ceiling twenty-seven times in a row — a record — then got down on the floor and did a headstand for a minute and thirty-four seconds. Finally, he saw the problems. Three things needed sharpening. From the word *survey,* Devillio might figure out that Adam was going to question kids at school. Also *parent.* That could be dangerous. Devillio might remember that Adam had complained about parents doing kids' projects. And *scores.* Too specific. Adam didn't want

Devillio wondering exactly which scores were being looked at.

He played and played with it and finally came up with:

A STUDY OF THE RELATIONSHIP BETWEEN
ADULT SUPPORT AND STUDENT ACHIEVEMENT

He kept saying the words in his head. Nice and scientific. Exactly what he'd be doing. Yet they kept his secret.

Before science class, he showed the title to Jennifer. "This sound OK?" he asked.

She read it a few times—he could see her lips moving over the words. "No offense," she said, "but I don't have a clue what it's about."

"Yes!" Adam cheered.

"You," Devillio hissed, and a chill went through Adam. He'd called attention to himself—what a fool.

"Can't you see I'm on my cell?" Devillio said. "Quiet down. Your abstracts are due. Pass them to the front. Then get out your nervous-system packets. I'll be a minute." And he disappeared into his office.

As the abstracts moved from the back to the front desks and as they slid across the front desks to the last desk on the right, Adam watched his disappear into a large, anonymous pile. It was like a game he used to play with Danny. They'd try keeping an eye on an autumn leaf until it blended into a larger pile and was lost.

His abstract was gone, one among many now, never to be read again, he hoped.

He pulled out his To-Do list and crossed off the abstract. He was feeling lucky. Shadow was next.

Adam went looking for Shadow at lunch but didn't find him. He kept walking by 107A, but the door was always closed. After school, he raced out to the pickup area looking for the small special-ed buses, but missed them. An aide said those buses left early so those kids wouldn't get trampled by the rest of the school.

Shadow really was a kid in the shadows.

Then it dawned on Adam. The Rec Center. Shadow had said he worked for some guy, Mr. Johnny Something, at the Rec.

As often as Adam had been there for swim team,

he had never been in the Rec offices. He waited to ask the lady at the front desk where he might find this Mr. Johnny Something. She was checking pool passes and was swamped with everyone rushing in. Kids in groups of two and three came jumping out of vans, SUVs, and Humvees and were streaming by, swim bags over their shoulders, boys and girls, from elementary to high school, laughing and horsing around. It was so busy that Adam had to wait several minutes.

The woman told him the offices were around back; there was a separate entrance Adam didn't know about. You had to go outside and behind the building.

It was a miserable winter night, moonless and freezing cold. The north wind blew through him, and it occurred to Adam that even if Bernoulli's inverse windchill phenomenon was a total fraud, he missed it.

That wasn't the only thing he missed. He walked all the way around before realizing he'd missed the back entrance. The doors were metal, painted blue, the same color as the cinderblock walls and hard to pick out in the dark.

He knocked, but no one answered, knocked

again, then squeezed the latch to open the door. He stepped up three stairs and into a room with several old, dirty metal desks, all unoccupied. It felt like a sauna—he could hear the rumble of the boiler, which had to be running twenty-four hours a day to heat the pool. "Hello," he called. "Hello."

Nothing.

Walking down a hallway, he poked his head into each room. These were empty, too. The rooms needed painting and looked like they were furnished by the Salvation Army—a mix of chipped metal desks, beat-up armchairs, and ratty sofas. Bags of sports equipment were piled in corners. The offices smelled like a men's locker room—musty, with a strong whiff of deodorant that delivered twenty-four-hour protection. The only clean items were the calendars, which were identical in every office. From an ad at the top, they appeared to have been furnished by Tookey Berry's Billiards & Paintball Emporium and featured a summery photo of a pretty lady with only half a bathing suit.

Finally, at the fourth office, Adam saw him. Shadow was sitting on a busted sofa that was tilting to one side—as was Shadow. On his lap was a stack of blue papers, and he was asleep. All around were piles of envelopes, arranged in neat stacks. Shadow had apparently been stuffing envelopes for a mailing. Adam gently picked up a blue notice from his lap. It was about a swim meet in March. Somewhere in those piles was an envelope stuffed by Shadow and heading to Adam's house.

Adam plopped down in an armchair across from Shadow and waited.

A door slammed several offices away, and Shadow opened his eyes. Without lifting his head, he picked up a blue paper, folded it in thirds, stuffed it in an envelope, and placed it in the proper pile.

Adam didn't want to scare him, so he softly said, "Noticing anything about how neat the piles are?"

Shadow blinked at Adam, then looked up like he was searching for a hole in the ceiling. "You weren't here," Shadow said. "Are you in a dream?"

"No," said Adam. "You fell asleep. You were sleeping when I walked in."

Shadow nodded. "Napping on the job is not a good habit to get into," said Shadow. "But do not worry. Mr. Johnny Stack says when it comes to a hard worker like you-know-who, it's no problemo, baby, the county's getting its money's worth."

"I have no doubt," said Adam. "You work harder than any kid I know. Actually, Shadow, the reason I came is I wanted to apologize."

"Why are you apologizing?" asked Shadow. "Did you fart? I didn't hear anything. If no one hears it, you don't have to apologize; you can pretend it wasn't you. Was it you?"

"No," said Adam. "I was apologizing for something bigger."

Shadow nodded and was quiet for a moment. "Because you didn't guess," he said. "It wasn't polite."

"That's right," said Adam. "Even worse, when you were trying to tell me something important, I didn't listen."

"That's right," said Shadow. "I had something important, and I am an important somebody. Mr. Johnny Stack says you'd have to be a fool not to see that."

"A fool am I," said Adam. "But I'm trying to do better. Look, Shadow, it took a while, but I think I did get your point—that your brother was one of the kids who stole my shoveling money?"

Shadow nodded.

"I appreciate it," Adam continued, "but I have to tell you, you shouldn't be talking about it to me. There's a court case, and you don't want your brother getting in more trouble."

"No problemo, baby," Shadow said. "My brother is already in more trouble. He's been in more trouble for a long time. My brother is in more trouble with me, too. He beat me on my head with a pipe. Really hard. He doesn't like me even though he's supposed to by law 'cause he's my brother. He says I'm a big mental case. He says it's my fault we lived in so many foster houses and no one wants to adopt us. He said, 'No one's going to adopt a retard.' He hit me on my head. Really hard. I got fourteen stitches."

Adam got a sick feeling. This creep was really bad news.

"Did you ever get fourteen stitches?" asked Shadow. "Want to see my scar? It's not too scary. My hair hides it."

"That's OK," said Adam.

"You won't have to get fourteen stitches," Shadow said. "My brother is in jail. Mr. Johnny Stack said he screwed up one too many times. Mr. Johnny Stack said this time they threw away the key."

Shadow tossed an imaginary key over his shoulder. "Mr. Johnny Stack said that's one less punk walking the streets."

Adam felt relieved. This must have been what Shadow was trying to tell him at the basketball court—that his brother wouldn't be bothering Adam anytime soon.

"I don't like him even though he is my brother," said Shadow. "We don't live together, ever since I was a little snapper."

"Little snapper?" Adam repeated. Shadow was like an unstoppable force, kind of like Phoebe. Once he was set in motion, you had to wait for him to run out of gas. Adam wasn't surprised Shadow's life was hard—just the way Shadow dressed and even from his smell, you could guess. But Adam didn't want to hear every detail. It was too sad. "Does Mr. Johnny Stack call you a little snapper?" Adam asked.

"Mr. Johnny Stack calls me Theodore. He says, 'That's your Christian name; that's what we're going to call you. Period.' My caseworker called me little snapper. She was my fourth caseworker. Her name was Miss Daisy, like the flower, always stayed an extra hour. Nice lady. I had nine so far. You want to hear? I can say all their names." He held up his fingers to count. "Mrs. Coley was roly-poly. Mrs. Ritter with two *t*'s was there one minute then gone like the breeze. Mrs. Scolli with an *i* . . ."

"Geez," said Adam. He thought of world history class again, those epic poems that the Greeks made up so they could remember all their heroic battles. That's how Shadow's life sounded, as many battles as the Greeks.

"You can rememberize anything if you rhyme it," Shadow continued. "It's a trick. A good trick. You want to hear everywhere I lived? That's a poem, too. Number nine, Highland Road, I lived there when I was one years old. Number twelve, Harbor-view—"

"You lived there when you were two," said Adam.

Shadow looked stunned. "How do you know?" he asked. "Did you live there?"

"A guess," said Adam. "Shadow, you're amazing."

"I know," said Shadow. "Mr. Johnny Stack says I'm Amazing Grace, except my name is Theodore."

"Mr. Johnny Stack coming back soon?" Adam asked.

Shadow explained that Mr. Johnny Stack was gone for the day. "It is perfectly OK for me to stay in his office until the Rec closes at ten," said Shadow. "A safe, warm place on a cold night—"

"I got to go, Shadow," said Adam. "I've missed most of swim practice. I need to duck my head in the pool so I smell like chlorine before my folks get here. Look, how can I find you at school? I went hunting for you today but couldn't find you."

"You went hunting for me?" Shadow said. "Was I missing?"

"Nope," said Adam. "I just wanted to know in case I had something to tell you. When's your lunch?"

Shadow had first lunch, with the elementary kids; he said he didn't change rooms like most kids, just stayed in Room 107A all day.

Adam hoisted his swim bag over his shoulder. "What time you getting picked up?" he asked. "It's late."

"I don't get picked up," said Shadow. "I walk."

Adam asked the address and recognized it as the Willows. "That's pretty far," said Adam.

"No problemo, baby," said Shadow. "One-point-three miles exactly. Mr. Johnny Stack measured it in his van. We watched the numbers go up. Tenths are in the little box at the end. They go faster than miles.

Mr. Johnny Stack says you can walk four miles in one hour if you don't dillydally. So 1.3 miles is way less than one hour."

"If you don't dillydally," said Adam.

"That's right," said Shadow. "Did Mr. Johnny Stack tell you, too?"

chapter 11

Upward and Upward

"There's no need for this," said Jennifer. "I Googled 'tree-falling deaths' and got 16.4 million hits. I have plenty of information to make my decision."

"That's exactly what's wrong with news today," Adam shot back. "Editors and reporters spend way too much time indoors. They surf the Web and think they've visited real places. . . . *Put your foot there.* Sometimes I feel like there's only four people in the entire country who go outside and do stuff and everyone else is online, posting comments about them. . . . *No, over there, grab that. Put your hand there. Now pull.*"

"This won't change my mind," said Jennifer. "Ow! I scratched myself. See?"

"You'll live," said Adam. "Come on, a little more. It's worth it, I swear to God."

"Why are you swearing to God?" said Jennifer. "You never go to church. You are such a hypocrite, Adam Canfield."

"Oh," said Adam. "So God only listens to people at church, you know that, right? *The other foot—put the other foot there.*"

"That's it—I'm not going any higher," said Jennifer. "We have so much work. You just want to get out of it. I'm heading down. My hands are freezing."

"Look," Adam said. "You're almost there. Please. Just look around. Smell the air. *Put your foot on that branch, your hand on that one. Now swing over.* You did it! I just wanted you to get to here. You can see everything. Lean back. It's great this time of year, with the leaves off."

Jennifer was quiet, finally. If this didn't convince her Phoebe's tree story was worth saving, nothing would. It was almost dark; they could still see their breath in the cold. Lights were coming on all over town. From up this high, they could spy the red lights of a cargo ship moving down the Tremble River and the green lights of buoys bobbing on the river and the boatyard all lit up with white head-lights from pickups and SUVs arriving for the night shift. A train was pulling in from the city. People were coming home from work. Cars were turning into driveways. Houses were lighting up.

"Geez," said Jennifer. "I didn't know. It looks so cozy and dreamy. Like a magic village."

"This tree's older than the country," said Adam. "I bet Indians sat where we are now."

Jennifer nodded. "I get it," she said.

He pounded his fist against the trunk. "Doesn't sound hollow to me."

"Hope not," Jennifer said quietly.

He grabbed the branch overhead and let his feet go, dangling, his arms fully extended. "Does not feel like a tree that's about to fall down," he said, swinging back and forth.

Jennifer gasped. "Stop!" she said. "You're scaring me."

Adam put his feet back on the branch. He noticed how tight she was holding on. "How come you never climbed it?" he asked. "I thought every kid did."

"I'm afraid of heights," said Jennifer.

Adam looked at her. "Whoa," he said. "This is a funny time to mention that."

"Look," said Jennifer. "I'd rather die of fear in this tree than hear you say one more time that I'm this typical editor spending too much time indoors."

"Jennifer," he said. "I didn't mean you. I meant typical editors in general."

"You did so mean me," she said. "And I don't ever want to hear it again. I'm plenty outdoors, and it's not even my story—it's Phoebe's." Jennifer gestured so dramatically, she lost balance and let out a shriek. Panicking, she flattened her body against the branch, wrapping her arms and legs tight around it.

"You OK?" asked Adam.

"No," said Jennifer.

"I think it's time to go down," he said.

"You go without me," she said.

"Listen," said Adam. "If I don't get you down, your parents will kill me. And worse—I'll have to work alone with Phoebe."

"Would serve you right," said Jennifer. "It would be worth dying, knowing that at least I got something out of it."

"Let's go," said Adam.

"I can't," said Jennifer. "I think I'm paralyzed with fear."

"Can you stick out your tongue?" asked Adam.

Jennifer stuck out her tongue.

"Can you say, 'Poopy-doody, poopy-doody'?"

"Poopy-doopy, doody-poody."

"Close enough," said Adam. "You're definitely not paralyzed with fear. You're just very scared. Hold on." He climbed down past her.

"Where you going?" she asked.

"Relax," he said. He moved directly under her and put his right hand on her right ankle. "It's an old Boy Scout trick," he said. "Loosen your right foot. . . . Good . . . I'm going to guide it to the branch below. No—don't look down. Look straight ahead. And when you feel your foot on the branch, you'll lower your weight onto it."

Back on the ground, Jennifer brushed all the twiggy dirt from her jacket. "Thank you," she said.

"No," he said. "That was really nice of you. I didn't realize—"

"It's OK," she said. "Have we been outdoors long enough?"

"Yup," Adam said.

"It wouldn't be a reporting violation to go some-place warm, would it?"

"Hot chocolate's on me," said Adam.

Jennifer pulled out a piece of paper. She was writing something.

"See?" said Adam. "It's paying off. You're making some reporting notes, aren't you? I knew it!"

She handed him her pen and the paper, which was folded. "Hold this," she said, bending over to undo her bike lock.

Then she yelled, "Race you to the Pancake House!" and bolted off. Adam grabbed his bike, but as he jumped on, there was a tug and he couldn't go anywhere. Jennifer's lock was still on his bike and he didn't know her combination! That weasel. For a minute he waited for her to come back. Then he realized. He slowly opened the paper she'd handed him. It had her combination and one word:

PSYCHE!

He should have left her in the tree.

/////

When he got to the Pancake House, Jennifer was already in a booth. "Get lost?" she asked.

"You are a riot," Adam said. "Last time I save your life."

"Let's not forget what genius almost got me killed," she said. "Truce? We got forty-five minutes. I called my mom; she's bringing my tennis stuff and cello. I'll change in the van."

Adam felt like a man of leisure. School basketball was over, and baseball practice didn't start for a few weeks. He was down to two winter teams— swimming and club basketball—and neither was practicing tonight. All he had tonight was a baritone lesson, at seven thirty.

The restaurant was pretty empty—just a few older people there for the early-bird specials. The coeditors ordered grilled cheese sandwiches and hot chocolates, and Jennifer pulled out her list.

For the tree story, Adam suggested they do a simple article saying that the state would be holding a hearing in March to determine what to do about dangerous trees. And the story could mention that one of the trees that could be cut down is the beloved three-hundred-year-old climbing tree. Then they could quote one of Phoebe's recycling friends talking about

143

how tragic it would be to lose that tree. And then they could get a comment from state officials about how they'll decide which trees to cut down.

"And then," said Adam, "we go to the hearing in March and figure out what's really going on."

"Fine," said Jennifer. "I like it."

"You know," said Adam, "Phoebe's story might turn out to be an iceberger."

"Iceberger?" asked Jennifer. "That's good?"

"The best," said Adam. "You know how someone calls you up and says, 'I finished reading your story on the tree and it's good, but it's just the *tip of the iceberg*!' And then they tell you some important secret, like the real reason the state wants to cut down the tree is blah-blah-whatever. That's an iceberger. A story that helps you get below the surface and find new information for your next story."

"Smart," said Jennifer. "Only one problem."

"Phoebe," said Adam. "I thought of that, too. We tell her that a lot of the great material from her first story—like the first twenty-three graphs—might go in the next story in March. We tell her this will mean two front-page stories in two months. And then we go with her to the meeting to make sure she doesn't mushroom out of control again."

"You'll do that?" Jennifer asked.

"I thought you would," Adam said.

Jennifer handed him the story announcing the *Slash*'s First Annual Bully Survey. "It's done," she said. "Read it when you get a chance; let me know if you have anything."

"You know how I feel about this," said Adam.

"Come on," she said. "Everyone wants it." The ballots would be full-size paper, she said, so kids could write in their worst bully experiences.

"Here we go," said the waitress, setting down the sandwiches.

"I'm starved," said Adam. But before taking a bite, he grabbed the ketchup and squeezed out an enormous glob on his plate. Then he took half his sandwich, dipped the tip in ketchup, bit off the part covered by ketchup, then dipped again and took another bite.

"Geez," said Jennifer. "Have a little ketchup."

Adam ignored her. Girls didn't know how to eat the right way. "So, how you going to make sure people vote just once?" he asked as thick drops of ketchup fell from his sandwich.

"Election monitors," Jennifer said. After a person voted, the monitor would cross off the name from the school list. "We'll do it in 306. Get people from the *Slash.*"

They started making a list. Adam said he knew a boy who'd make a good monitor. "He never forgets a name or number." He opened his mouth to tell Jennifer, then stopped.

"Ketchup clog your vocals?" Jennifer asked.

"Theodore," Adam said. "The boy's name is Theodore."

They were dreading the Dr. King story. Neither wanted to do battle with the Bolands, Tremble's most powerful family—owners of one of the biggest cable companies in the nation—along with various and sundry Boland businesses, including Boland Realtors, Inc.

"We can't get out of it," said Adam. "A church full of black people protesting a street named for Dr. King is too amazing."

"Yeah," said Jennifer. "Too bad it's all off the record."

"Remember what Reverend Shorty said when I asked the date of the protest?" Adam said. "'Don't think we'll have to.' Why wouldn't they have to?"

"That was off the record, too," said Jennifer.

"And the nine boarded-up houses," Adam continued. "I totally believed his theory." Reverend Shorty had told them that the Bolands planned to buy all the houses they could in the Willows, not just the nine. They'd board them all up, make the neighborhood look terrible, and get people to move away. And then, Reverend Shorty said, Boland Realtors, Inc., would bulldoze the Willows and put up million-dollar mini-mansions for rich people. Goodbye, Willows. Hello, Boland Estates.

"You know," said Jennifer, "I'm sure Reverend Shorty's right, but it's just his theory right now. And it's all off the record."

"That stupid rainbow ceremony," said Adam. "It's just the Bolands pretending they care about the Willows when they're out to destroy it."

"Another off the record—"

"*Stop!*" yelled Adam. "*Would you stop saying it's off the record? I know it's off the record. I was there. Just stop! Stop!*"

147

The restaurant went silent. Old people who'd been happily eating the $4.95 liver and onions special were staring in horror at Adam.

"Don't worry, folks," Jennifer said looking around. "He gets very emotional sometimes. He's not dangerous or anything." She put her head close to his, and though her voice was a whisper, Adam could see she was smoking.

"I thought you were different, Adam Canfield, but you're such a typical . . . typical . . . *boy*," she hissed. "You're always pressuring me to do what you want! I'm sick of it. You're trying to pressure me to shut up by talking louder than me. You pressured me to go up that tree so I'd change my mind on Phoebe's story. You pressured me to kill the bully survey. You even pressured your way into this Dr. King story. I didn't ask you to come along."

Pressure? thought Adam.

"Pressure!" said Adam. "Jennifer, you're a genius. That's it! That's the answer to Reverend Shorty's riddle. He doesn't have to protest; he just has to put *pressure* on them by threatening to protest. I bet anything he pressured the county *and* that Bleepin school guy big-time by threatening to march if they didn't call off the ceremony. That's why they don't have a date. Reverend Shorty pressured them into backing down.

"That's our story for the February *Slash*: they're not going to rename that street. Schoolchildren won't be going to a rainbow ceremony. Everyone's too afraid of a Dr. King protest at the Dr. King ceremony. It's dead."

"OK," said Jennifer. "Now, please don't take this the wrong way, but what's our source?"

"Notice I'm talking in a very calm, very low-pressure voice?" said Adam. "Our source is you. You've got every name we need in your notebook from last week's board meeting. Lots of people will be telling us the ceremony is off. And Dr. Bleepin, too. It'll be a new experience for him. He's going to tell us the truth."

"Why would he do that?" asked Jennifer.

"Because we're going to trick him into it," said Adam.

What a relief. They'd meet after school the next day to finish reporting. They still didn't know what to do about the boarded-up houses, but they'd worry about that for the March issue.

"Sound OK?" asked Adam.

"Fine," said Jennifer.

"Not feeling too much pressure?"

"I'll be all right."

Jennifer's mom was waving in the window. It was time to go.

Adam started getting up, but Jennifer grabbed his arm. She handed him a pile of napkins. "Clean the ketchup off your face and the table," she said. "You're scaring the old people. You look like the lead story on the six o'clock news."

Outside, Adam helped Jennifer lift her bike into the van.

"I can take yours, too," Jennifer's mom said. "Bring you home after I drop Jen at her lesson."

"It's OK," said Adam. "By some mess-up, no one scheduled anything for me until seven thirty. I think I'll bike to the Rec and see a friend. See if I can get him to join the *Slash*." Then Adam waved, did a curb grind, and was gone.

"Is he all right?" asked Jennifer's mom. "Looks like someone bloodied his face. Does he get mugged a lot?"

"Just grill-cheesed," said Jennifer. "Adam's definitely all right."

chapter 12

Getting Used
to Getting Used

Jennifer sat on a newsroom couch. In her lap was the notebook from the last school board meeting. She'd gone through and circled several names. Beside her were the Tri-River Region white pages.

Adam was working the phones.

"Try this one," she said, handing him another number.

"It's ringing," Adam whispered.

"Hello and *hola*," said a man. "This is Javier Freedman of the Perfect Mix. We sing for one and all."

"Hello," said Adam. "I just want to make sure I have the right number. You guys are the educational singing group?"

"Exactly!" said the man. "As featured on Boland Channel 12's *Community Miracles*."

Adam told him he was a reporter for the Harris *Slash*.

"Oh, I love student newspapers," said the man. "Such a force for enlightenment. How can I help, Adam?"

Adam explained he was doing a story on renaming the street for Dr. King. "I was just wondering what songs the Perfect Mix will be singing."

"Aren't you a gem," said the man. "Unfortunately, Adam, it's been canceled."

"Oh no," said Adam, trying to sound sad, even though he was jumping up and down and pumping his fist so hard, he might have dislocated his collarbone.

"What?" Jennifer mouthed.

"It's been *canceled*," Adam repeated. "But we were really looking forward to it."

"Weren't we all?" said the man. "I don't think I ever remember a single event in Tremble history that was going to be so multicultural. . . ."

"You're sure it's been canceled?" asked Adam.

"We had a call from the zoning board."

"The zoning board," said Adam. "Mrs. Boland's zoning board canceled it?"

"That's right," said the man.

Adam got the spelling of his name, thanked him, hung up, and turned to Jennifer. "That's one source," he said.

She had another number waiting. From her notes, she remembered about the ten kinds of sushi they planned to serve at the ceremony and figured the caterer had to be Huck Finn's California Sushi De-Lite Restaurant, the number-one sushi distributor for your office or home party needs in the Tri-River Region.

This call took less than a minute, once Adam got the catering manager. The guy told Adam his name was Sal You-Don't-Need-to-Know-No-Last-Name. He said the King thing was off; he said that he "didn't have no freakin' clue why." Then Sal hung up.

"Two sources," Adam said to Jennifer. "We're out of here."

"To Bleepin's office," she said.

They tossed everything in their backpacks. As they were hurrying out, Adam said, "You got your color-coded calendar with you?"

Jennifer froze. "How do you know about that?"

"Trained observer," said Adam.

"How long have you . . ."

Jennifer kept a daily calendar of her activities, all color-coded. Geography Challenge was green, Quiz Bowl Gladiator blue, cello brown, tennis purple, club basketball black, *Slash* meetings pink. Adam had known for a long time, but he'd been saving it up. It was one of those perfect pieces of information you could use if you ever needed to torment someone.

Now he felt bad. He'd waited too long to use it against Jennifer. He really did have a good reason for bringing it up.

"It's for the story," he said. "I swear. I'll tell you on the way over."

The district office was in the same complex as Harris Elementary/Middle, but on the other side of the ball fields. It took ten minutes to walk.

Jennifer explained to Bleepin's secretary that they were from the *Slash* and though they didn't have an appointment, they were on deadline and had a few questions they hoped to ask Dr. Bleepin about Black History Month.

154

"We know Dr. Bleepin is a real kid person," said Adam. "Our deadline for the February issue is a few days off, and we thought we'd take a chance dropping by."

The secretary said she'd peek her head in and ask.

While the woman was gone, Jennifer said, "What was that about Bleepin being a kid person? You don't know that. Why do you throw stuff like that in?"

"Everyone in education's a 'kid person,'" said Adam. "Reporters just say that to establish their expertise. It doesn't mean anything. The higher up these guys are and the fewer kids they see every day, the more they're a 'real kid person.' I'm just getting on this Bleepin guy's good side."

The woman came back and said Bleepin would be delighted to meet; he just had to finish a call.

That was Jennifer's cue. She pulled out her calendar. "Excuse me," she said to the secretary. "I'm such a scatterbrain. They have us so busy, I have trouble keeping up with all the stuff I'm supposed to do. I keep this calendar—"

"It's color-coded!" said the secretary. "Ohhh, is that adorable. You kids—you're really something. I don't know how you do it. They've got you so scheduled. If I was a kid today, I think I'd crack up."

"I know what you mean," said Jennifer. "Look, I'm nervous. We're supposed to cover this ceremony for Dr. King's street. I always put special events like this in harvest gold." And here Jennifer wiggled a harvest-gold pencil from her sixty-four-pencil set at the secretary. "I was wondering if you know when that's going to be. I'm worried I'll miss it. If I can color-code it in on my calendar, it calms me down."

"I am so touched by your little calendar," said the secretary. "And it is wonderful seeing a young person so interested in her heritage. Unfortunately, that ceremony is not going to happen. There were . . . um . . . problems."

"Problems?" said Jennifer. "I hope nothing, you know . . . racial?"

"Oh no, honey," said the secretary. "Nothing like anything racial. No, no, no. Cross that off the list. Absolutely not racial. To be honest, I don't know what it is. But it's the people in the Willows who don't want it."

"Really?" said Jennifer.

"Really," said the secretary.

"Really," said Adam, who dropped his pen so he could bend over and secretly write down her quote.

Jennifer sat back down. "Guess I won't be needing

this," she said, giving her harvest-gold pencil one last friendly wiggle at the secretary before sticking it in her pencil box beside sunrise yellow.

Then she whispered to Adam, "Three sources."

"So glad you dropped by," said Dr. Bleepin. "You know, I'm a real kid person. It's wonderful to see a couple of actual kids close up. Reminds me what this is all about." He lifted a mug of coffee and saluted them. "So what can I do to you? Ha, ha."

"We were wondering why the Dr. King ceremony was canceled," said Adam.

Coffee came spraying out of Dr. Bleepin's mouth in every direction. "You what?" he gasped.

Adam repeated it.

"Where did you hear that?" said Dr. Bleepin. "Nobody said that. Don't you say I said that."

"Everybody knows," said Adam.

"Let's see," said Jennifer. "We spoke to that singing group, the Perfect Mix, the one you were raving about at the meeting . . ."

Dr. Bleepin stared at them.

"And Sal the sushi man, he said it was off," said Jennifer. "And your —"

"Well, we're not supposed to say that," said Dr. Bleepin. "We're supposed to say 'the celebration has been extended.' Let me get the exact words." He rummaged through papers and pulled out a printout of an e-mail. "We're supposed to say"—and here he began reading—" 'To ensure that everyone in Tremble's wonderful community partakes in this historic event, school officials have decided to extend—' "

"I'm sorry. Geez, could you please slow down?" said Adam. "If this is what we're supposed to say, we want to get it right. Could I just look at that for a second?"

Adam held his breath and extended his hand like it was perfectly normal for him to be swapping secret memos with a first-assistant-associate-superintendent.

"You want the memo?" Dr. Bleepin said. "Hmmm . . . the memo . . . all righty," and he handed it to Adam.

Adam could not believe it. What reporting! At that moment, Adam felt like there wasn't any piece of information he couldn't squeeze out of Bleepin. It made him wonder—was there a Reporters' Hall of Fame?

The *Slash*'s star reporter quickly skimmed the memo. It was from Mrs. Boland! That was huge. She was calling the shots, not school officials. But in the memo, she blamed school officials for everything. It made it sound as if Mrs. Boland's zoning board had nothing to do with messing up the renaming ceremony. Everything in the memo was "School officials were sorry . . ." "School officials regretted . . ."

Adam slipped the memo to Jennifer to copy.

"Dr. Bleepin," said Adam, "we were really wowed by you at the board meeting. I mean, that's why we're here. What a presentation!" Adam was laying it on thick. Feed the big guy's ego and get the news — that was Adam's motto. "But this doesn't seem fair," Adam continued. "Weren't there hundreds of petitions for this?"

Bleepin opened a drawer, hoisted a stack of papers, and thudded them on his desk. "Over a thousand signatures," he said.

"Wow," said Adam. "The people have spoken. Mind if we borrow these?"

"Be my guest," said Bleepin. "They're copies. The originals are with the county. They're public; anyone can see them."

"With all these signatures, how could they cancel it?" asked Jennifer.

"Check the addresses," said Bleepin. "Not one

from the Willows. The county used a couple stooges—two idiots named Herb, I think—and these Herbs got signatures in North Tremble and West Tremble, but not a soul from the Willows."

"Wow," said Adam. Bleepin was dazed, a deer frozen in Adam's headlights. The *Slash* Hall of Famer moved in for the kill. Adam opened his eyes wide and flicked on the high beams. "Dr. Bleepin," said Adam, "do you think it's a problem, not getting anyone from the Willows?"

Bleepin got up and walked around his desk, so he was towering over Adam and Jennifer. "Do me a favor," he said. "Stop talking to me like I'm an idiot. I know who you are. You're the two kids who got Marris fired."

Adam felt like he'd just been slammed against the wall. It was like Bleepin had grabbed the remote and changed channels in midsentence. They'd been cruising along on Disney, and suddenly they'd been switched to a reality cop show with a shaky camera.

"Pay attention," said Bleepin. "You've got what you need to write a story that says it was the county zoning people who screwed up this King thing, not the schools. You've got the cover-up memo from Boland, and, of course, you won't say where you got it."

They looked at him.

"And of course you won't say where you got it," he repeated.

They nodded.

"And the petitions," he said. "Public record. Same thing's in the county building. And of course you won't say where you got your copies."

They nodded.

He walked to the door and said, "See you."

"We might need some official comment," said Jennifer.

"My comment?" said Dr. Bleepin. "No comment."

They walked back to school to catch a late bus.

"That was great," said Jennifer.

"It was?" said Adam, who wasn't feeling great.

"Do you know what just happened in there?" asked Jennifer.

"Truthfully? said Adam. "I don't have a clue. I thought I knew exactly what was happening until we got to the end, and then everything changed so fast."

"We're being used," Jennifer said cheerfully.

That was good news? To Adam it sounded awful. One minute he thought he was squeezing out

Bleepin's deepest secrets; the next minute Bleepin was throwing documents at them.

"Reporters are always being used," said Jennifer. "Bleepin gave us that stuff because he doesn't want Mrs. Boland blaming everything on him. He's using us to attack Mrs. Boland."

"Is that fair?" asked Adam.

"It wouldn't be fair if we just printed Bleepin's side," Jennifer went on. "But we take everything we know, including Bleepin, and weigh it and then do the story."

"Being used," Adam said. "It makes me feel . . ." He didn't finish. It made him feel unimportant.

"Get used to it," said Jennifer. "Don't you ever watch C-SPAN? When the president's pissed at some senator, what does the president do? He gives a bunch of secret documents to a reporter that will make the senator look like an idiot. And then the reporter writes a story: 'Secret Documents Reveal that the Senator Is an Idiot!' Then, to get even, the senator takes his secret documents and gives them to a reporter, and there's another story: 'New Secret Documents Reveal that the President Is an Idiot!' Then they both start screaming, 'Someone has been leaking secret government documents to the press!

We need an investigation!' And then they show con-gressional hearings on C-SPAN: 'Plugging the Leaks, Day 24.'"

Adam nodded. "I guess," he said. "I was wondering—what do you color-code your C-SPAN viewing time?"

"Pale rose," Jennifer said.

"Got you!" yelled Adam. "You are sick. Color-code me out of here." And he raced off.

She hated him—she really did.

chapter 13

The February *Slash*

"Cookies?" said Mrs. Quigley, offering Adam and Jennifer a plate of Mrs. Radin's Famous Homemade Super-Chunk Buckets O' Chocolate Moisty Deluxe chocolate-chip cookies.

Boy, Adam loved Moisty Deluxe. He was thinking Mrs. Quigley must buy them by the case, the way she gave them out. Word was getting around Harris that being called to the principal's office wasn't that bad.

"My philosophy is 'Eating healthy twenty-four hours a day causes unhealthy stress,'" said Mrs. Quigley, who was munching a Moisty Deluxe herself. That was Adam's philosophy, too, but he eye-balled Jennifer to see what to do. After the Erik Forrest circus, Adam wasn't sure if these Moisty Deluxe might be an ethics violation.

He hated how complicated this ethics stuff was. Mrs. Quigley was really two people at once for Adam and Jennifer. She served as adviser for the *Slash*, and it probably was OK to eat Moisty Deluxe offered by your adviser, since you worked together putting out the paper.

But she could also wind up being someone they had to write about, making free Moisty Deluxe an unethical gift. What if they had to investigate her? What if those Moisty Deluxe were a cover-up, and she was stealing the children's money, like Mrs. Marris? She seemed nice, but one thing Adam had learned: Adults had secret personalities that they hid under their public, jolly selves.

"Thank you, Mrs. Quigley."

Jennifer, the Ethics Queen, ate a cookie! Adam was cleared. When the plate reached him, he grabbed three, since, as Mrs. Quigley correctly pointed out, he was a growing boy.

/////

Going over the final proofs of the *Slash* with Mrs. Quigley was way better than with Mrs. Marris. Mrs. Quigley hardly changed a thing, but that wasn't the best part. For a principal, she seemed like a newshound. They could tell she'd read every word and not just because she was looking for problems. She kept saying, "How'd you get Reverend Shorty to talk?" And, "I'm going to the Lido Deli and see if the bacon-egg-and-cheese really deserves 4.5 yummy-yummies."

She totally got Adam's piece. She said Erik Forrest sounded like a very nice man, but she certainly wasn't going to buy his pancake book.

And Jennifer was beaming after Mrs. Quigley said the bully story seemed fine. The principal said bullying was a serious problem meriting front-page coverage.

Two stories were scoops, beating the *Citizen-Gazette-Herald-Advertiser*, TV-12, and the radio stations.

The front-pager about naming the street for Dr. King ran under the headline "King Street Dead-Ends!" Jennifer and Adam both got bylines.

Mrs. Quigley said she was impressed with all their digging, and Adam had to admit that even though Jennifer was an editor type, she was making good progress with investigative reporting thanks to his steady guidance.

Jennifer did not stop after the interview with Bleepin. Next, she called back Reverend Shorty and told him everything they'd discovered. He was most impressed with the Mrs. Boland memo. "Where'd you get that?" he asked, but of course, Jennifer could not say. Until Jennifer's call, Reverend Shorty had not even known the ceremony was off; no one from Mrs. Boland's office or the schools had called him.

Even so, Reverend Shorty still did not want to go on the record, until Jennifer squeezed him.

Jennifer explained that Dr. Bleepin's secretary told them the ceremony was off because the people in the Willows did not want it.

Jennifer explained that the story could stop there. But then, she said, readers might think people in the Willows didn't like Dr. King. "You know," Jennifer had said, "Adam and I looked through the petitions and we didn't see one signature from the Willows. You could give us a quote on that."

And he did. The Jennifer squeeze worked as sweet as fresh orange juice from the blender. Reverend Shorty's quote talked about the need for the county to consult people in the Willows *before* making changes to the Willows. He also noted that Willows residents would be happy to meet with the county to discuss any "future issues affecting where our people live."

Jennifer knew what that meant: the houses boarded up by Boland's real estate company and the pressure on Willows residents to move away. She tried mightily to get Reverend Shorty to say more, but that was as far as he'd go. No more fresh juice.

"If your article turns out good, we'll talk again," he said. "Those Bolands say we're a 'pocket of blight.' They claim they got to eliminate the Willows to beautify Tremble. I've got lots to say on that. But we need to be careful. The Bolands have all the power. They can squish you like a bug."

The other scoop was the three-hundred-year-old climbing tree.

As predicted, Phoebe was a total train wreck

when she heard that the coeditors insisted on a much shorter story.

Phoebe said she couldn't think of a single word, not one, that could be cut out without ruining everything and demanded that they take off her byline.

But, as Adam predicted, she calmed down once she realized she'd have two front-page stories in two months. "No third grader," Jennifer said, "has ever produced so many front-page stories in one year."

"Really?" Phoebe said. "Not even your coeditor when he was in third?"

"Nope," said Jennifer, who wasn't sure, but needed to get the tree story in the paper sometime before they *all* turned three hundred.

After much persuading, Phoebe called the state people. A spokesperson e-mailed a statement acknowledging that the climbing tree was one of several under study but emphasized that no decision had been made. And though this was the last piece of information collected, it became Phoebe's lead:

> Tremble's beloved 300-year-old climbing tree could soon be cut down under a new state program aimed at eliminating

dangerous trees before they fall on people,
a state official told the *Slash.*

Jennifer even got Phoebe to take a photo of the tree without Phoebe in it. The story ran on the top left of page one:

CLIMBING TREE
SOON TO BE
300-YEAR-OLD
WOOD CHIPS?

Even Phoebe liked the headline. "Sounds like a haiku," she said.

Adam was right about another thing. After the *Slash* came out, Phoebe got lots of calls from tree lovers saying that her story was good as far as it went, but *it was just the tip of the iceberg!*

Phoebe was in heaven. Notebooks full of secret info began piling up on her desk. After a while, whenever Adam or Jennifer picked up the phone and it was for Phoebe, they'd call out, "Iceberger, line two!" One afternoon, while lying on a newsroom couch reviewing her secret files, Phoebe fell asleep, and a kid put a sign on her that said CAUTION, ICEBERG CROSSING. And if someone was making a McDonald's run, even if Phoebe wanted chicken nuggets, they'd always put her down for an "ice-burger."

Mrs. Quigley visited several delis that week, then sent Sammy a note saying that she found his bacon-egg-and-cheese ratings "scientifically sound." The story was a big hit. Kids who couldn't care less about the Dr. King story memorized every rating. Letters to the editor poured in; everyone had an opinion on bacon-egg-and-cheese.

The Lido Deli asked for permission to put Sammy's 4.5 yummy-yummies review in the window, which Jennifer said was fine. However, she nixed the deli's offer to supply two dozen free sandwiches. In the past Adam would have joined the mob of *Slash* staffers throwing things at Jennifer, but since the Erik Forrest story, he was with her.

/////

Adam's Erik Forrest story ran at the bottom of page one under the banner "Celebrity Profile: Erik Forrest." The story started on a harsh note:

> Why would one of the great war corre-spondents write a stupid book about being a Mr. Mom for six months?
>
> "You know why I did it?" Erik Forrest said. "I figured, 'This is going to be the easiest $200,000 I ever made.'"

But as the article went on, it became clear that Adam liked Mr. Forrest. He talked about how kind Forrest had been to give a student reporter an exclusive. He talked about how Forrest's war stories could touch a person's heart. He described Forrest's comments about what it took to be a great reporter and how that was what Adam tried to do, too.

Adam mentioned how much Forrest knew about great writers like Dickens, Kafka, and Faulkner. He described how Forrest was scared his third marriage might fail and then concluded by saying that writing a book that was unimportant in order to try to save your marriage was a lot better than getting drunk and writing bad movies or burning your books, like other famous writers.

As requested, Adam mailed a copy of the article to the address on Mr. Forrest's business card.

But without question, the biggest splash of the February *Slash* was the story announcing the bully survey. It ran page one, top right, and was the talk of the school. Kids' only complaint was they'd get just one vote.

They loved the chance to write down their favorite bully story.

No one was more excited than the newest *Slash* member, Theodore "Shadow" Cox. The coeditors had made Shadow official fact-checker and already Shadow had proved his worth.

He caught a math error in Sammy's bacon-egg-and-cheese formula that nearly gave several delis an extra three quarters of a yummy-yummy.

Shadow saved Adam from writing *Erik Forrest* as *Eric Forest*.

And Shadow noticed that the story on Dr. King had mixed up two Willows streets.

When a *Slash* staffer asked what he was working

on for the next issue, Shadow said, "I will be official fact-checker, reporting directly to the coeditors, checking all official facts for the bully survey. That's it."

And when kids asked how he liked the *Slash*, Shadow said, "I found seven mistakes so far."

The staff was glad to have him — except Phoebe. Every time Phoebe was alone with Jennifer, the world's greatest third-grade reporter would drop it into the conversation. "That new guy," Phoebe would say. "The official fact-checker. He's weird."

"Relax," Jennifer said. "He's nice. You'll get used to him."

"I don't think so," said Phoebe.

Adam and Jennifer were convinced that the real thing upsetting Phoebe was that there was now someone on the *Slash* as weird as she was.

Wherever Adam went, kids asked about the bully survey. They wanted guarantees that the vote would be secret. One wanted to vote for himself.

Several claimed that Adam had created the survey to get back at the kids who stole his shoveling money, to make himself look like a big antibully star.

Adam denied it, but when they insisted, he let it go. He didn't bother explaining that he was the only staffer who voted against the survey. It didn't matter anymore; he could live with it.

But a week after the *Slash* came out, something happened that did worry him. Mrs. Quigley showed up in 306 and asked to speak with the coeditors alone. She said since the *Slash* had come out, she'd been having second thoughts about naming the top ten bullies. She said a lot of grown-ups she respected said it might be unfair to single out troubled kids who were still only in middle school. She said she still felt the poll would be useful for school officials to identify the worst bullies, but after the results were in, she might ask them not to print names. "You know I love a free press," she said. "I'm sure we can work this out." And then she gave them a smile that reminded Adam of Mrs. Marris's do-it-or-die smile.

Adam was worried that he was getting his first glimpse beneath the public-jolly Quigley to the true-hidden version. The real Mrs. Quigley appeared to be seeping out.

chapter 14

A Surprise Visit

Adam was making great progress on his science fair investigation. He'd drawn up surveys and gotten one hundred kids to fill them out so far. His goal was three hundred, which would be half the seventh and eighth grades. He had them do it at lunch, a table at a time. At first it was hard. They complained that they spent their whole day working like dogs and the last thing they needed at lunch was filling out a stupid survey. But when Adam told them it could mean that they would never have to do the science projects at home again, they got into it. Plus, the survey was anonymous and supposed to be secret, so that made it seem a little dangerous.

Adam asked kids to use a scale of 1 to 5, to rate how much their parents had helped on last year's project: 1 was not at all; 2 was somewhat (helped with up to one-fourth of the project); 3 was moderate (helped on half the project); 4 was a lot (helped on three-fourths); 5 was REALLY a lot (helped on every step, from finding an idea to creating the poster display). Then he asked for their grades on last year's project.

He drew a graph in his science binder to plot the results and each day added dots from the latest lunchtime surveys. On the x-axis (the horizontal line of the graph), he had the 1 to 5 "Help" ratings. On the y-axis (the vertical line) he had the "Grades." The first time he plotted the results, he let out a whoop. They made a near-perfect 45-degree line heading up to the right. His hypothesis appeared correct: the less help a kid got, the lower the grade; the more help, the higher the grade. Kids who said they got no help clustered mainly between failing and the mid-70s; kids who said they'd been helped somewhat ranged from high 70s to low 80s; kids who got help on half the project were bunched in the mid-80s; and kids who got lots of help—4s and 5s—scored 90 to 100.

It wasn't perfect. There were a few who got a lot of help and scored in the 80s. And a few got no help and scored in the 90s. Those kids Adam was in awe of; they should have won the fair.

But the more surveys he added to the graph, the more they confirmed the trend: more help equals higher scores.

Adam thought that could be the headline when he wrote up the results for the *Slash*.

Through it all, Adam tried to be as invisible as possible in Devillio's class.

Two things made him feel hopeful.

When he got back his abstract from Devillio, it had a check mark and just one comment: *Font too large. Use 16 point.*

No way Devillio had read it.

A few days after that, Devillio called on him. "Please hand these tests back, son," he said.

He'd forgotten Adam's name. Invisibility was key when battling the Devil.

The only people who sensed something fishy were Adam's parents. They kept saying it was time for the family to get started on his science project. When Adam told them he wouldn't need help, his mother looked shocked. "You sure?" she said. "You may be the only one."

Adam was in the back of the newsroom with Shadow, working on his survey sheets. Shadow was reading off numbers, and Adam was plotting them on the graph when the door to 306 opened.

"So, this is the *Slash*," said the woman. "I've heard sooo much about it."

Room 306 went silent. They were good journalists and they could feel it: menace in the air. Kids who'd been slouched on a couch, instinctively jumped to attention. A girl lying flat across the top of a desk executed a flawless dismount. Phoebe discreetly gathered all her top-secret notebooks and stuffed them in a drawer.

After the voice came a thick perfumey smell that made Adam sneeze. This was no ordinary adult. And she was not alone. Mrs. Quigley was by her side.

"Boys and girls," said Mrs. Quigley. "We have an important visitor today. Mrs. Boland is here, and guess what? *She* has news. As you may know, Mrs. Boland is a very busy woman. She's chairperson of the zoning board. She's director of the Boland Foundation, which donated the study guides for the state tests free of charge. And along with her husband, Sumner, the Bolands own the *Citizen-Gazette-Herald-Advertiser,* Cable News 12, Boland Broadband . . ."

Mrs. Boland was smiling as if no one knew better than she did what a big shot she was. Adam edged back against the wall, hoping to stay out of her line of vision. As Mrs. Quigley spoke, Mrs. Boland's piercing green eyes scanned the room, like a searchlight hunting escaped convicts. Adam was sure he knew the names of the escapees. Only when her beam moved away did he dare look at her.

She was prettier than he'd expected. He would have guessed that up close, she'd be plastered with makeup to cover her monstery self, but the truth was that her skin looked soft and clean and she had on a black business suit that Adam had to admit made her look, well, good in a curvy kind of way. Her hair was different from when he'd seen her on TV for Peter Friendly's ten-part series on zoning scourges. It was shaggy, with blond and black streaks—a lot was going on but that didn't look bad either. Adam was surprised; Mrs. Boland looked good enough to be on Tookey Berry's Billiards & Paintball Emporium calendar.

"Mrs. Boland has come with exciting news," said Mrs. Quigley. "Would you like to tell them, Mrs. Boland, or shall I?"

Mrs. Boland made a sweep of her arm as if to say she was way too modest to honk her own goose.

"Of course," continued Mrs. Quigley. "Mrs. Boland is launching a massive countywide beautification program. School playgrounds and parks will be renovated. Ball fields will get new grass, fencing, and lights. New trees will be planted."

Mrs. Quigley explained that to announce this exciting news, Mrs. Boland was touring the schools. "And guess what her first stop is?" Mrs. Quigley paused dramatically. If they were grown-ups, they would have known this was the moment to clap to show their infinite gratitude to Mrs. Boland for choosing Harris Elementary/Middle to launch her beautification tour. But they were kids, and even worse, newspaper people. And because they were readers of their very own *Slash,* they knew that this was the woman, in person, who had tried to tear down every basketball hoop in Tremble during her last beautification binge. Even the littlest were not fooled.

Mrs. Quigley had rolled a ticking time bomb into 306.

From the corner of his eye, Adam saw a blur of motion, and then realized that it was Jennifer, hurrying up front. "That is so nice," Jennifer said, clapping as she walked, which got them all clapping.

The principal gave Jennifer a big smile and mouthed the words "Thank you," then introduced her to Mrs. Boland.

"Ah, yes, Jennifer, I recognize the name," said Mrs. Boland. Trying to be professional, Jennifer offered her hand, but Mrs. Boland ignored the gesture, as if touching anything Boland was a huge deal.

The woman's search beams were still scanning for the other escapee. "Aren't there supposed to be two of them?" she asked.

Mrs. Quigley looked puzzled.

"Editors," said Mrs. Boland. "Two editors."

"Ah, yes. Adam," said Mrs. Quigley. "Adam."

Adam was under a desk, supposedly looking for a pen top.

He stood slowly and walked up front. "Found it," he said, waving the pen.

Mrs. Quigley said she was sure that the *Slash* would want to do a story about the beautification plan, and she noted that Mrs. Boland had insisted on coming up to 306 to give the reporters the scoop in person.

"Wonderful," said Jennifer. "But Mrs. Boland, we know how busy you are helping people, so if you want to leave us a press release, we'll write it up. . . ."

"Darn," said Mrs. Boland. "Did I forget that press release? Maybe we could do a little interview."

The bell rang.

Adam had never seen kids load up backpacks and scoot out of a room so fast. The only sound was everyone murmuring, "Excuse me, excuse me," as they piled out.

That was Adam's plan, too. "Got to go," he said, hoisting his baritone. "Geography Challenge and baritone lesson."

"Adam," said Mrs. Boland. "I'm sure the *acting* principal would excuse you from class for a few minutes. This won't take long."

"No problem," said Mrs. Quigley, heading out the door. "The two of you just stop by my office when you're done. Mrs. Rose will give you late passes."

"Mrs. Quigley . . ." Jennifer called out, and Adam could hear the fear in her voice. "Would you like to join us for the interview, Mrs. Quigley? You might have ideas . . ."

"I'm sorry," said Mrs. Quigley. "I'd love to, but the kindergarteners are taking their state coloring proficiency test. I'm a monitor and as usual, I'm late." She winked at them and disappeared down the hall.

The door clicked shut. They were alone with the time bomb.

"Well," said Mrs. Boland. "At last."

"Would you like to sit down?" Jennifer asked.

"In this sty, are you kidding?" said Mrs. Boland, and she shuddered.

"It's great about the beautification plan," said Jennifer, who was struggling to keep things on the surface. "I was wondering —"

"Please stop," said Mrs. Boland. "I'm going to make this fast. I should have closed you down after that basketball story. Don't think I couldn't have. One call to the right politician — good-bye. But no, I figured you're just kids, you've got basketball hoops at home, you're too lazy to go to the park, so you write some slanted story against me. I let it go. My gift to you. But isn't it human nature — you do people a favor, you think they thank you?" She shook her head. "No, no, no. They think you're soft. First opportunity, they cram a stick of dynamite up your behind."

"Mrs. Boland," said Adam, "we appreciated it. I don't know if you saw the quote—"

"You don't have a clue," said Mrs. Boland. "I've worked so hard to protect this community from becoming another suburban wasteland overrun by chain-link fences, above-ground pools, and aluminum siding. Do you know what I get paid as zoning board president? Zippo. I donate my salary to charity. My gift to the people of Tremble. I hire renowned experts and develop a master plan to keep Tremble a lovely place for good people who work hard and earn a good living. I could quit and settle for having a 'nice' suburb, but that's not me. I won't rest until we're the jewel of the Tri-River Region. And what thanks do I get? I get a story in your paper about people in the Willows not being consulted on changes to their crummy, run-down neighborhood. Not being consulted!" Mrs. Boland slammed a desktop.

"My God, the dust," she mumbled, pulling out a wipe from her briefcase and cleaning her hands.

"Since when is the Willows your problem?" she went on. "You like it so much—I don't see you living in the Willows. You live in River Path," she said, pointing at Adam. "And you," she said to Jennifer. "Every night your daddy comes home from his big-city law firm to that nice house in River Bluffs."

The coeditors looked stunned.

"You think I don't know about you?" Mrs. Boland continued, riveting her beam on Jennifer. "Your folks don't go to church in the Willows. They go to that nice big church in North Tremble."

"You, I understand," she said, nodding at Adam. His shirt was untucked. His hair was standing up in back. His shoes were untied. "What a mess," she said. "I can see you'd be right at home in this slop bucket. But you," she said to Jennifer. "You seem to have been raised with manners and style. Surely, young lady, you understand that being a clean, orderly person and living in a clean, orderly town go hand in hand."

"It's my fault," said Adam. "Jennifer tried to get us to clean up the newsroom."

"Please stop," she said. "You are done writing about the Willows. You hear me? It would be so easy to shut you down. I could be shocked to hear that the *Slash* has no full-time adviser. Your poor acting principal is so busy. So we at the Boland Foundation could provide you an adviser from my beloved husband's *Citizen-Gazette-Herald-Advertiser* to watch over you, day and night. A mentor to edit your stories so they turn out right. Make sure you baby reporters don't get confused. Clean stories to help beautify Tremble.

"Or I could get a bunch of managers from Bolandvision Cable, people my husband pays generous salaries to, so they can afford the taxes that fund your schools. And they could come to the school board and demand to know how, in this time of scarce resources, Harris can afford a whole room for a student paper plus the cost of publishing monthly. Wouldn't it be sad if we needed to make cutbacks? Slash the *Slash* from the budget.

"You give it some thought. See if you need any more stories on the Willows."

Mrs. Boland stared hard at them. "That will be all," she said.

Adam felt like he was coming down with bubonic plague.

As Mrs. Boland wheeled to leave, he got a whiff of her perfume again, and—he couldn't help it— sneezed twice this time.

She froze. Adam could see her shudder. "Didn't

anyone ever teach you to cover your mouth?" she snapped.

"Mrs. Boland," said Jennifer, "you never told us about your beautification plan for Harris."

"Silly me," she said. "You know what's funny? I do have those press releases." She reached into her briefcase, yanked out a thick stack, crumpled one, and threw it in Adam's face. "Special delivery," she said, and turned to go. But as she slid the releases back in, she fumbled and dropped her briefcase.

Adam bent to pick it up, and Mrs. Boland gasped.

"Please, no," she said. "Don't touch that with your sneezy hands."

She pulled a handkerchief from her sleeve, used it to lift the briefcase, and marched out.

Neither Adam nor Jennifer spoke for a long time. They'd never felt so cornered by a grown-up.

"My God," Jennifer finally said. "I could barely breathe."

"I know," said Adam. "She was, like, worse than Marris, she was like . . ." The two looked at each other, neither able to think of the words.

"What was that deal with the wipes and the handkerchief?" said Adam. "She seemed like a clean freak."

"Clean hands and a clean county, I guess," said Jennifer. "Are there any normal grown-ups?" She picked up the crumpled press release and smoothed it out.

"Don't waste your time on that," said Adam.

"Oh my gosh," said Jennifer. "Reverend Shorty was right." She showed him the end of the release. It said the new beautification program would make an all-out effort to eliminate Tremble's last "pockets of blight."

"That's their code for the Willows," said Jennifer.

"It doesn't actually say Willows," said Adam.

"It means Willows," said Jennifer.

chapter 15

A Second Surprise Visit

Adam needed to talk to Danny, and it wasn't just this Boland mess.

The judge's clerk had called Adam's dad about the shoveling case. The judge wanted to hear from Adam about the mugging and any feelings he had about how the five arrested kids should be punished. Community service? Counseling? Jail? Lethal injection?

In a case like this, the clerk explained, the victim's feelings were given weight.

Adam's feelings? His feelings were that he didn't want to get involved. That was the judge's job. That's why judges had those big gavels—not to kill bugs — but to slam down and say, "Three years hard labor. Next!" Adam had never seen anything on TV about *victims* being given the gavel. What if people found out that he'd recommended jail? He never realized how much went into being a victim.

His dad said Adam didn't have to make a recommendation and shouldn't worry about it.

But Adam wasn't sure. Adam really wanted to talk it out with Danny.

Adam wanted to find out if Danny knew Mrs. Quigley.

And, more than anything, Adam needed help figuring out what to do about the Willows story. He didn't want to discourage Jennifer. She'd never done such great reporting. But maybe it wasn't the job of a school paper to write about the Bolands buying up the Willows. That was grown-up stuff. Kids wanted to read about the top ten bullies. They wanted egg sandwiches.

Danny had been a huge help when Marris was after them.

Only one minor problem.

Adam had to find Danny.

/////

Saturday morning, after baseball practice but before running club, Adam rode his bike to the animal shelter.

The receptionist told him the same thing she'd said when Adam phoned: Danny wasn't in. And no, she didn't know when he'd be back.

"I'm his really good friend," said Adam, "and I'm worried about him."

"You're so lucky to have Danny for a friend," she said. "He's amazing when he's up."

They always said that about Danny. She made it sound like Danny lived in an elevator. "When he's up?" repeated Adam. "Where is he now? Down?"

The receptionist gave Adam a strange look but didn't say more.

"Do you know if he's all right?" asked Adam.

"We know he's OK," said the receptionist. "He checks in with us. It's just—I can't say more for privacy reasons. Please understand."

Was Danny on some secret animal shelter mission? Maybe he'd gone undercover investigating a poodle smuggling ring in Paraguay. Adam wasn't even sure they had telephones in Paraguay.

"I really need to talk to him," said Adam. "But he's never home."

"You sure?" she said. "Look, I've already said too much. People are waiting." Adam was so absorbed, he had not noticed. Behind him were a woman and a little girl with a pet adoption form. Behind them was a man with a golden retriever and a lady with a white boxer.

This was his parents' fault. He hated them for not letting him have a dog. They kept saying he was too busy and would never walk it. He hated being so overprogrammed. He'd love to quit swimming. He'd love to quit before-school/after-school classes for the state tests. He'd love to have just one second to himself.

He stepped out of line. The little girl was telling the receptionist that she was going to adopt a Yorkie terrier and call him New. "Everywhere I go I can tell the whole, entire world, I love my new Yorkie, New. Get it? And in a long time, when I get growed up, I can say I love my old Yorkie, New. Get it?"

Adam got it. Couldn't one thing on this entire planet love him twenty-four hours a day for no good reason except that he was Adam?

Being a reporter, it seemed like he spent every waking hour asking questions that upset people. He wasn't sure how much longer he could stand the reporter's life. He wanted to be surrounded by love and get licks all over his face every second.

It was too far to bike.

He didn't know which buses to take.

And Adam didn't want to ask his parents for a ride; they'd start getting snoopy about what was up.

So that Sunday afternoon, a glorious March day, Adam waited until his mom and dad went biking along the river. He opened his desk drawer, pulled out forty dollars from his savings, and called a taxi.

Usually, Danny came over to their house. Danny wasn't married, and Adam's parents said they enjoyed cooking for him. Adam had been to Danny's only twice. Danny lived in a condo; that had surprised Adam. It was pretty plain and not too large. For some reason Adam had envisioned Danny in a more dramatic place, like a houseboat on the river or a bat cave.

The taxi driver knew the condo complex and Adam showed him which building. He felt funny standing there, watching the taxi disappear. Only then did it occur to him—what if Danny was in Paraguay?

Adam pressed the buzzer for Danny's condo. There was no answer. He pressed two, three, four times.

There was a rustling over the intercom. "Yeah?"

"That you, Danny? It's me, Adam. . . . Danny, it's Adam . . . your friend, Adam. . . . Danny?"

Finally Danny said, "It's not a good time for me. How about if I call you when it's better? Put your dad on, I'll tell him."

"I'm alone, Danny," said Adam. "I really need to talk to you."

There was another long silence. Then Danny said he'd buzz him in, but Adam had to wait ten minutes in the lobby before taking the elevator up.

When Danny opened the door, he barely looked at Adam. No bear hug like usual. No jokes about how much Adam had grown. No comments about the beautiful Jennifer. No nasty remarks about Adam's ridiculous, overprogrammed life.

Danny looked bad. He needed a shave, and what hair he had on the side of his head, was sticking out, Bozo-style. He was wearing a white T-shirt and sweatpants, and though it was late afternoon, he seemed like he had just gotten out of bed.

Usually Danny was rushing around so much, he crackled with electricity. Today, he looked unplugged.

The apartment was a mess. Even Adam noticed. Old newspapers were piled everywhere—the *New York Times, Wall Street Journal,* the *Tri-River Post-Gazette.* Dirty dishes filled the sink and kitchen counter. It was unbelievably hot and stuffy.

"It's burning in here," Adam said. "Feels like a hundred degrees."

"Didn't notice," Danny said softly. "You think I should open a window?"

"Might be good," Adam said.

Adam tried to make chitchat about the animal shelter, but Danny gave one-word answers. The man looked like he couldn't get comfortable. He sat in the center of the couch, staring down, his hands clasped in his lap. Or he got up and paced back and forth across the living room. Then he'd lay back on the couch, his head propped on a pillow for a minute before getting up again and pacing.

Finally, Adam could not ignore it. "Geez, Danny, are you OK?"

"No, I'm not," said Danny.

"What's wrong?" asked Adam, who suddenly was scared. "You don't have anything like cancer? Oh please, no," he blurted.

Danny shook his head. "Nothing like that," he said. "Physically, I'm healthy as a horse."

"Great," said Adam, although it didn't seem great.

Danny continued pacing. "Look, Adam," he said. "I hate people seeing me like this. I've got this illness. . . ." He stopped.

"Illness?" asked Adam. "I thought you're healthy as a horse."

"Physically," said Danny. "It's the head. Adam, you know. . . . Let me see how to say this. . . . You're probably too young. . . ." Danny's head was in his hands now. "You should go . . . please."

He paused. Adam stared at him. Danny lay back on the couch. His arm was over his eyes. He was quiet a long time. Adam was determined to wait this out.

"Mental illness," Danny finally said. "Ever hear of that?"

"Sure," said Adam. "Like when people are crazy."

"Well, I have a mental illness," said Danny.

"That's ridiculous," said Adam. "You're, like, the neatest grown-up I ever met. Even Jennifer says so. You know all kinds of stuff, you know lots of good jokes, you like kids, you listen, you got that great job at the animal shelter. You've got the record for most pet adoptions in a day. Even you said, 'Forty-nine, a record never to be broken in our lifetime.' Danny, you seem like the least crazy grown-up I know."

"Right," Danny said. "Well, I set the record when I was up. And I'm down now. I couldn't do a single adoption right now. That's why I'm on leave. It's my illness, Adam."

The phone rang, but Danny didn't move.

"Want me to get it?" asked Adam.

"I don't care," said Danny. Adam walked to the phone and checked the caller ID. "Tremble Animal Shelter," Adam read. Danny shook his head.

"They told me you check in every day," Adam said. "Let them know you're OK."

"I leave a message after it's closed," said Danny. "I really think you should go."

Adam didn't budge. He'd worked too hard tracking down Danny. "What's your illness?"

Danny gave him an irritated look, but Adam stared right back.

Danny took a pillow from the couch, put it on the floor, then lay down on the floor. "It has different names," Danny said. "Manic depression is probably most honest. Mood swings. Up and down. The brain's chemistry is all screwed up. Doctors don't even understand it."

"They don't give you medicine?" Adam asked.

"Meds, oh yes, miracle meds," Danny said. "I take every last med they give me. It doesn't make you better. Helps a little around the edges. I can go months, sometimes more than a year being up. And then, down. Months of being down. Months of depression."

"You're depressed?" said Adam. "Is that all? Why didn't you say so? Come on, Danny, cheer up — you're the best. After I was mugged, I was kind of down, but I got out of it. Think of good stuff. Like all the skips we've had by the river." Adam was thinking of how for years the two had gone down by the river a couple of times a year to skip rocks. "You want to go get an ice cream? It's beautiful out."

"It's not like that," said Danny. "It's not something where you can be cheered up. You could eat a thousand ice creams, but your mind can't feel the joy of ice cream. You're numb. Dead inside. It's like the brain's ability to absorb happiness has been turned off. Click."

Adam thought about that. "Well, how do you turn it back on?" he asked.

"You wait," Danny said softly. "Take your meds and wait. For as long as you can bear it. If you can bear it."

The phone rang and again Adam checked. The caller ID said *Dr. Rieder*.

Danny grunted but held out his hand for the portable. As he talked, he rubbed his forehead. Adam heard snatches of conversation as Danny walked in and out of the room. "On a scale of ten? Three. . . . No, I don't think I need to go in. I really don't. . . . I actually met my social goal today. I have a friend over for a visit. . . . Yes, I do . . ." The rest was mostly *yes*es and *no*s. Adam was sure of one thing: Danny talked a lot less when he was like this.

When Danny hung up, Adam said, "I guess I'll be going."

"OK," said Danny. "I appreciate it."

Adam put on his jacket, then asked if he could borrow the yellow pages to look up the taxi number.

"Taxi?" said Danny. "Is that how you got here? A taxi? Alone?"

Adam nodded.

"Does your dad know you're here?" asked Danny. Adam shook his head.

"I forget," said Danny. "Why did you come?"

Adam explained that he'd wanted Danny's help. For himself and for some *Slash* stories. "It's OK," said Adam. "I didn't know you were mentally ill. I'll just ask someone else."

For the first time Danny looked at Adam like he used to. "You're telling me you came all this way in a taxi by yourself? To ask *me* for help? Me? Oh, you beautiful child. Put the phone down. Come here." Adam walked over and Danny gave him a big hug. Adam was crying now, and when he looked up, so was Danny.

"I'm sorry, Danny," Adam said. "I'm sorry I made you more depressed. I didn't mean to make you cry. I'll go."

"No," said Danny. "Oh, no. I'm feeling something. It's so wonderful to feel something."

Danny made Adam call his dad, who insisted on coming to pick Adam up and said he'd be there in forty-five minutes.

When Adam got off the phone, he noticed that Danny had a glass of water and was taking pills. "Every six hours," Danny said. "I apologize ahead of time—they make me drowsy."

In the past, when Adam had asked Danny for help, the ideas popped out rapid-fire and Adam could barely keep up. This time, Adam had to go slow, and even then, Danny had trouble following, so Adam had to repeat some stories.

Adam asked about their new principal, but Danny didn't know Mrs. Quigley. Danny did seem interested in two things that Adam had barely given a thought: that Mrs. Quigley was the *acting* principal, and that she seemed like a grandmother.

Danny said this might be very bad news. It might mean she'll be at Harris a short time and will do whatever she is told. It might mean that if Mrs. Boland wants to destroy the *Slash*, Mrs. Quigley will look the other way, collect her paycheck, and be gone at the end of the school year.

Or, Danny said, it might be good news. It might mean that Mrs. Quigley's a seasoned pro, doing Tremble officials a favor filling in while they search for a permanent principal. And since Mrs. Quigley might not be worried about her bosses, she could be independent enough to do the right thing. "In my experience, only two groups of people speak the truth," said Danny. "Kids and old people. Kids don't know better; old people have nothing to lose. You might get lucky with this Quigley woman."

Adam liked that idea. It had never occurred to him that a principal might be brave. "Every time we meet," said Adam, "she gives us Moisty Deluxe and milk."

Danny shook his head. "Can't trust cookies and milk," he said. "Even Moisty Deluxe. It could be taken either way." Adam knew Danny was right. The moment Mrs. Marris had started smiling like crazy at Adam and Jennifer, that's when things had turned into a nightmare.

Adam looked at the clock; they'd used up half an hour. He didn't know if it was his imagination, but Danny seemed to be moving in slow motion now. He'd stopped pacing and was lying on the couch. He kept saying he was sorry, that his mind didn't work when he was depressed, and he had to ask Adam to explain things a second and third time.

After hearing the latest developments in the shoveling case, Danny agreed with Adam's dad — it probably wouldn't go to trial. The boys would most likely plead guilty, Danny said, and the penalty would be a lot less than the four years mentioned on TV.

But Danny thought Adam should go to court and make a recommendation about the sentencing. He felt it was Adam's duty. "You called the police," Danny said. "They came. The district attorney, the judge—they're part of a system that's there for you. The court system is one of those things that separates us from cavemen. Everyone needs to do his share. You, too."

By the time Adam got around to the Bolands, Danny's eyes were closed. It was almost dinnertime and the room was nearly dark. Adam's dad would be there any minute.

Danny's answers were shrinking. Adam wasn't even sure he was awake; sometimes it was like he was talking in his sleep.

Adam told Danny about the Bolands boarding up houses in the Willows. Every few sentences, he had to ask if Danny was listening. And Danny wouldn't even open his eyes. He'd just lift one hand off his stomach and make a slight wave.

"My big worry is this isn't a story for a kids' paper," said Adam. "I mean, kids don't care about this stuff. So I think I'll tell Jennifer we shouldn't do it. That sound right, Danny . . . ?

"Danny . . . ?

"Danny . . . ?"

"Kids live in the Willows?" Danny whispered.

"Sure," said Adam. "You know they do."

"They go to Harris?"

"Yeah," said Adam.

"What if they disappear?"

"Disappear?" said Adam, "Why would they disappear?" Danny said nothing and Adam was quiet, too. Disappear? Disappear! "I get it!" Adam shouted. "That's our peg—the kids. Tell it through the kids. Oh, that's great. Danny you're unbelievable. You're like this sleeping oracle. You're like Superman fighting with his last ounce of strength before the kryptonite gets him. . . . Danny? . . . Danny?"

Danny did not answer.

Adam flopped in a chair. The room was dark, the only sound Danny's snoring. Adam sat there, barely visible between the tall stacks of newspapers on each arm of the chair, waiting for his dad to buzz.

chapter 16

Democracy

On the way home, Adam's dad grilled him about taking the taxi to see Danny.

Adam told the truth, but not the whole truth.

Adam did not mention asking Danny for advice about the shoveling case. He did not want his parents thinking he was going behind their backs and trusting someone else.

Adam did not say anything about the stories he was working on. If his parents knew he was preparing to do battle with both Mrs. Boland *and* the Devil, his mom and dad would yank him out of Harris and homeschool him in the basement.

All Adam said was that he was worried about Danny being depressed.

It worked.

Half the truth was plenty.

His dad was amazed Danny had seen Adam. "When Danny's down," his dad said, "he won't even see me. You really are something, Adam. I'm very proud of you."

Adam nodded and stared out the window. He loved his dad. For an adult, his dad really tried hard to figure out what was going on.

After dinner, Adam grabbed the portable and went to his room to call Jennifer. He told her all about his visit to Danny. He explained to her that he had been worried about the Willows story not being right for a kids' paper. "But Danny solved that problem. He's amazing," said Adam. "It's more work for us. We're going to have to—"

"Talk to kids in the Willows," said Jennifer. "Guess who I chatted up? Tish Osborne."

"Where'd you see him?" Adam asked.

"I had my tennis lesson," she said. "And my mom was late afterward. I was killing time, watching the boys play basketball."

"And you asked him?"

"One of the things," she said.

Jennifer said Tish had heard his mother talking about the boarded-up houses. "Tish said people are nervous. He said a kid he knew lived in one of the houses. And after the Bolands bought it, the family couldn't find another place in the Willows to rent and couldn't afford anything close by and wound up moving someplace far away, like outside Tremble. Tish couldn't remember where."

"Wow," said Adam. "That's exactly what we need. Can we use that in the story?"

"I didn't ask," said Jennifer. "We were just talking about personal stuff. I would've felt funny. Tish can be kind of touchy."

"He seems a little mean," said Adam, "but he did me a couple of huge favors. He's a pretty surprising person."

"You know that?" said Jennifer. "*You're* a pretty surprising person. I've known him a long time. We were together four years in a row in elementary. He acts so above everything, but he's definitely got another side. Like that day at Pine Street Church, watching over the little boys."

Adam felt bad; he'd never thanked Tish about getting his ball back. He owed Tish.

"He's really smart," said Jennifer. "But I don't think he ever takes home a book, just gets by. The boy can play ball, though. Football, too. And is he hot or what?"

Adam had lost track of the conversation. He'd been following it fine until the part about Tish being hot. He'd never noticed anything about Tish being hot. What was that? How did that get into the conversation?

"Adam, you there?" asked Jennifer. "Adam, come on. There's no need to get mopey. You know Tish likes that Ashley Wheatley," said Jennifer. "She's a lucky girl. . . ."

Mopey? Why would he get mopey? A lucky girl? So that's how it went. Jennifer just happened to be watching the boys play basketball. Right. They were just talking about personal stuff. Right. Adam had seen a few reality shows; he knew something about how the world worked. Jennifer was trying to deny everything, make a big deal about Tish liking this girl Ashley. As if that meant Jennifer couldn't be liking Tish, too. *Ashley is a lucky girl. Tish is hot.*

"The girl goes out with the second-hottest point guard on the team . . ."

Adam couldn't listen to another second of Jennifer's malarkey. He had this terrible, empty feeling. He didn't even remember saying good-bye. He tossed the portable on his bed, picked up his books, and trudged down to the computer. There was nothing worse than Sunday-night homework.

And Tish was the second-hottest point guard?

Adam froze. Tish was the SECOND-hottest point guard?

He instant-messaged Jennifer. *Did you say Tish is SECOND??? hottest point guard?* he typed.

Did I? she typed.

You did, he typed

Oh my, she typed.

Don't lie, he typed.

Good-bye, she typed.

/////

210

It was midnight by the time Adam finished studying for Devillio's unit test on the nervous system. Adam memorized the three types of neurons. He memorized the difference between a receptor and an effector. He knew that the trochlear was the nerve that controlled the superior oblique muscle of the eyeball and that the glossopharyngeal was the nerve that controlled the tongue muscle. He could fill out every line of the diagram showing what part of the brain controlled smell, speech, muscle movement, skin sensation, convulsions, and vision. The only thing he didn't know was how his brain always managed to hold on to every last one of these dopey definitions and multiple-choice answers until he'd taken Devillio's test and then instantly forget it all.

Oh well, he didn't have a clue how his brain worked, but was thankful to have one that got As.

After turning off the lights, he lay in bed trying to hold on to the feeling of Tish being the second-hottest. It faded fast. His worries, on the other hand, would not fade. He wondered if Tish would talk to them for the *Slash*. Was Mrs. Quigley on their side or against them? And worst of all, Mrs. Boland. If they did the Willows story, they'd have to see her again.

He'd show her this time. He'd spruce himself up so neat and clean, she'd be stunned. The thought of seeing her close up made Adam shiver, and he tugged the quilt up to his chin.

Adam was out front in the running club race, heading down the homestretch. Not a cloud in the sky, and he'd never noticed, but today, every blade of grass on the track's infield was perfectly trimmed, like a putting green. The white lines separating each running lane were exact, right down to the last white-chalk molecule, which, come to think of it, Adam could see clearly now, thanks to his new microscopic vision. It was fun having microscopic vision, and he was glad his parents gave it to him for Christmas.

He had about a hundred yards to go, when the second-hottest runner started closing the gap until the boy was right on Adam's heels. Speaking of heels, his new microscopic vision had detected tiny clumps of caked mud on the bottom of his running shoes. Adam was trying to clean the shoes and run at the same time, when the second-hottest runner whizzed by, then the third-, fourth-, and fifth-hottest. The race was over. Adam was last.

Head down, he waited for someone to say that he had nothing to be ashamed of, but nobody did, and Adam started limping a lot so everyone could see that finishing last wasn't his fault; it was his leg's fault.

And then, with no warning, in the center of that perfectly clean infield came a mammoth explosion, and there stood a terrible vision. It was curvy and shaggy on top, and was gleaming so brightly it appeared to have just climbed out of the bath tub. There were fiery green eyes, and each one had a blinding beam pointed right at Adam. And the beast bellowed, "You're obviously a pig. You tracked mud onto my clean infield—prepare to die!"

Adam searched for some way to fight back, but the infield was so clean, there wasn't even a twig. Desperate, he could think of just one thing. He yanked off his running shoe and heaved it with all his might toward the fiery green eyes.

Adam crouched, covered his head, and, as instructed, prepared to die. There was a roar and shriek. "No, no! Not those tiny clumps of caked mud!" the beast bellowed. Adam peeked up. The beast teetered, then collapsed, falling to the ground with a deafening thud.

The room was dark; the covers were on the floor. For a long time, he lay still, waiting for his breathing to return to normal. What a dream. He must be losing his mind. He had a feeling there was an important hidden message—that beast seemed awfully familiar—but then his head got heavy, and he was asleep again.

Next afternoon, the lines to vote in the bully survey snaked out of Room 306 and down the hallway. There was such a crowd, Mrs. Quigley assigned a security guard to the third floor. She said the last thing she wanted was kids bullying other kids about who should be worst bully.

The voting took longer than expected, and it wasn't just the large turnout. Kids spent a lot of time writing their favorite bully story. Some needed both sides of the ballot.

The coeditors had planned to have the voting in 306. But when the line backed up to the down stairway, they decided to hand out ballots to everyone waiting in the hall.

Kids sat right on the floor and filled them out.

To make sure everyone voted just once, the coeditors assigned Phoebe and Shadow to be voter monitors. The two carried official Harris Elementary/ Middle School clipboards, which, for Phoebe and Shadow, was nearly the same as having super powers. As students handed in the folded ballots, the monitors checked off the names from the school attendance list and asked for each voter's birthdate to confirm that no one was using another kid's name.

More than half the school voted. While Adam still thought the survey was a bad idea, even he got caught up in the excitement. *Slash* staff members felt on the inside of something very big. They loved walking in and out of 306 whenever they felt like, without having to stand in line.

Phoebe would deny it to her grave, but Adam calculated that she had walked in and out of 306 a total of 107 times, just for the power of it. At one point, to torment her, Adam suggested that she stay in the hallway and they'd let her know if she was needed inside 306.

"Can't do that," Phoebe said. "I'm on strict orders from your coeditor, Jennifer, to make sure that all is going smoothly on *both* sides of that door," she said, pointing to 306 as if it was Saint Peter's gate. "If you have other orders, please clear them with Jennifer, the *Slash* senior coeditor."

Senior coeditor? Phoebe really was cheesy. Adam could not let her get away with that. "As a matter of fact," Adam lied, "Jennifer herself told me she wanted you to stay out here in the hall. Jennifer said."

"I'll need that in writing from Jennifer," said Phoebe. "A lot of rumors are going around, and as Jennifer herself told us during our monitor briefing, we don't want to be faked out by some quote-unquote idiot. No offense."

In the end, Phoebe got hers.

Her official comonitor nearly drove her mad. The two were constantly bickering over who got to check off each voter.

"I saw her first," hollered Phoebe, racing to grab a fourth grader's ballot. Phoebe had taken off her shoes and slid the last ten feet down the hallway, narrowly beating Shadow to the girl.

"The coeditors said monitors are supposed to take turns," said Shadow, snatching the ballot from Phoebe. "You had the last turn. So I have this turn. Taking turns means you have a turn, then I have a turn. It does not mean you have a turn, then you have a turn, then I don't have a turn."

Finally Jennifer had to pull them aside and threaten to take away their clipboards. "I don't know if I can trust you with official school property," she said.

"That's not fair," said Phoebe, holding up hers. "I care! You see all these neat flower and butterfly stickers I put on mine? I'm not some kind of jerky person," and she stared at Shadow so there was no question which jerky person she meant.

"Neither am I some kind of jerky person who doesn't care," said Shadow.

Jennifer ordered them to keep track of how many each registered and make sure they did exactly the same number. "It would mean a lot to me," she said.

For the rest of the afternoon, Shadow shadowed Phoebe everywhere, reading off the totals after each ballot was collected. "That's 87 registered for you and 86 registered for me," Shadow announced. "Eighty-seven is one more than 86. So I register the next one. Then I will be 86 + 1, 87, and you will be 87 + 0, 87, exactly the same. And it will really mean a lot to Jennifer."

When the voting was completed, the *Slash* staff wanted to count the ballots immediately, but the coeditors nixed that. Adam and Jennifer worried that if all twenty-four did the counting, results would leak out prematurely. They said they would tally the ballots themselves, pick out the strongest bully stories, and report to the staff.

Adam and Jennifer each took half the ballots home. Adam couldn't wait to see the results. He brought the ballots to his room, closed the door, and dumped them on the floor. He would not have admitted this to Jennifer, but it was very exciting. There was a piece of him that really wanted these kids to be humiliated for being jerk-faced bullies. He was looking forward to calling Jennifer as soon as he had the totals. He wanted to see if they both got the same top ten. Then they'd add the votes together.

After the first couple of dozen votes, a clear leader emerged and as far as Adam was concerned, it was a great choice. This boy was awful. Part of what made his bulliness so aggravating was his phoniness. On the surface, he sounded great. He was tall and wide — muscular, not fat — a star on the football and wrestling teams. His folks owned a gas station and convenience store in town plus a copy store, and they were big deals in the Chamber of Commerce. Adam was always seeing their photo in the *Citizen-Gazette-Herald-Advertiser,* getting some kind of plaque.

Even so, this kid was the essence of snaky bulliness. He wasn't running around beating the crap out of everybody every second. It was more that he was constantly reminding kids, in quiet ways, that he could do whatever he pleased. He'd cheerfully mention that you were in *his* seat at the lunch table and make you move. Or he didn't want you sitting in the back of the bus just for today because he was saving seats for his friends. Or he'd pass in the hall, giving you a big smile and a playful punch on the arm that left a dark bruise.

Adam himself had voted for the creep.

But the pure joy of seeing a bad kid exposed had disappeared by the time Adam was half done counting.

One of the top ten vote getters—toward the bottom, maybe ninth or tenth, but still top ten—was Shadow. At first Adam thought it was a mistake, that kids put his name down because he'd collected their ballots. Then Adam had a moment of panic, worrying there was a side of Shadow he didn't know. After all, Shadow was strong—the work for Mr. Johnny Stack made the veins in his arms stick out. He was always lurking around. Maybe he had a crazy side Adam didn't know about.

But then Adam read the comments. *Room 107A drools the world,* one kid wrote. *Retard for president,* wrote another.

Shadow was their joke vote.

There was more discouraging news. A lot of kids got at least one bully vote, including Adam, who got three. He didn't know for sure, but he could guess which star third-grade reporter cast one of them. And while three votes was nowhere near enough to make top ten, he felt terrible. One kid wrote: *This whole bully vote is to scare kids because you're a chickenshit who called the cops for no good reason. Forty bucks is a joke!!!*

And there was worse news.

In second place when Adam stopped counting was Tish Osborne.

Tish, who made sure Adam got picked that Saturday on the Rec courts. Tish, who got Adam's basketball back and didn't hang around to be thanked. Tish, who helped at church. Adam was beside himself. These people who voted—they didn't understand a kid like Tish. They just saw the surface stuff. *They* were the jerks.

Adam kept thinking about what it would be like telling Tish that he'd been voted Harris's number-two monster.

He could not count another ballot. He didn't want to know the results. For a moment, he thought about ripping them all up and chucking them out.

He hoped Jennifer was happy. He'd told her this bully vote was a mistake. But did she listen? No one listened to him. She'd manipulated the whole *Slash* staff against him. Fine. Let her break the happy news to Tish. And Shadow — she could tell Shadow, too. That would be a great moment in modern journalism. Shadow didn't have enough problems.

Adam hated this. He felt some of it was his fault. If only he hadn't invited Shadow to join the *Slash.* If Shadow hadn't been collecting the ballots, kids would never have thought to vote for him.

Adam went into his closet and pulled out a shoe box full of basketball cards. He dumped the cards into the third drawer of his bureau, his sports shorts drawer. Then he scooped up the bully ballots, stuffed them into the empty shoe box, fastened the top with rubber bands, and shoved the box into the back of his closet, where no one ever looked, behind his black tie shoes.

chapter 17

Resigned and Unresigned

Adam had been looking forward to screaming at Jennifer about the bully survey. He wanted to yell real loud for about fifteen minutes until she got down on her knees and admitted in cold blood that she'd been wrong.

But when he actually got the chance, there was no joy in it. Jennifer was as miserable as he was.

"What are we going to do?" she kept saying, and each time, there was a noise that sounded sniffly to Adam.

Adam couldn't be sure it was sniffly. The boat dock was dark, and with the river lapping against the shore, and the dune grass rattling in the night breeze, he might be mistaken.

He was sure of this: the last thing he needed was a sniffly Jennifer. Jennifer was the rock in these life-or-death situations. She was the one who'd pulled Adam through those bleak days with Marris. She was the one who'd kept her cool when Mrs. Boland cornered them in 306.

"Why didn't I listen to you?" she said.

"I don't know," said Adam.

"We never should have done the bully survey."

"I know," said Adam.

"You tried to tell me, but did I pay attention?"

"You did not," said Adam. "Nope."

"I feel like a total failure."

"I bet you do," said Adam.

Adam waited for Jennifer to say the next stupid thing she'd done, but instead, she kicked him hard with her hiking boot.

"Ow!" he shouted. "That hurt."

"I hope you're bleeding," she said. "You're supposed to be supportive. We're coeditors. I'm doing my best here."

"I was being supportive," said Adam. "Everything you said I agreed with."

Jennifer was ticked. "You really are an idiot," she said. She looked at him and how the wind was blowing his hair. "We have a more basic problem here. You know what my mom says about middle-school boys? 'UPS never delivers the complete package. It can take years before the entire shipment turns up.'"

"We use FedEx," said Adam.

"I rest my case," said Jennifer.

Unfortunately, they did agree on one thing: this was an impossible mess. If they printed the bully poll, it would be unfair to Shadow and Tish. But if they *didn't* print the poll—it was like they were censoring Harris students, throwing out a fair election because they didn't like the results.

They needed a plan fast. While the bully poll wouldn't come out until the combined March/April issue, the *Slash* staff was demanding to know *now.* Phoebe alone had written seventeen e-mails marked URGENT RESPONSE REQUESTED. *Just finished brushing and flossing and thought I'd check once more before bed,* Phoebe wrote in e-mail number fourteen. *ANY NEWS??!!* And when Jennifer answered, *Not yet,* Phoebe e-mailed again in twenty minutes. *Decided to trim toenails and Q-Tip wax from ears. ANY NEWS??!!*

That's why they were sitting on the dock in the

dark. Even Phoebe wouldn't bother them there. They'd started at Adam's house, then walked up his street and along the river, stopping at a dock that belonged to summer people who weren't around.

Everything they considered had a bad side. They thought of destroying the ballots; removing students from the top ten list they felt weren't real bullies; naming only the first-place bully.

Maybe they could secretly ask Mrs. Quigley to kill the story. Hadn't she said she might do it on her own? And then they could deny asking her.

They discussed running a story admitting they made a terrible mistake and then not printing the bullies' names. Or they might admit they made a mistake and print the names.

Every choice had a terrible side. Destroy ballots? Alter results? Lie? That's what people like Mrs. Boland and Devillio did, not the coeditors of the *Slash*. Adam and Jennifer were supposed to be good guys. If they started messing with the facts, someone at Harris would have to start a second newspaper just to investigate them.

The *Daily Phoebe.*

Adam could think of only one way out.

What if he resigned as coeditor?

That alone would cut his To-Do list in half. He could see living the resigned life, full of lazy spring afternoons, running through fields teeming with dandelions and butterflies.

"Maybe I should resign," said Jennifer.

What? Did he just hear that? Had Jennifer read his mind?

"This bully thing was my idea," she continued. "You were against it. There's no reason for you to take the blame. If I resign, it gives us a way out. I could write a story saying I made a terrible mistake; I never dreamed the survey would turn out so mean; and instead of hurting innocent people, we decided to kill the story and I was resigning."

Adam shivered and it wasn't the river breeze. Jennifer resign? He'd thought of it first; he just forgot to say it out loud. Things were getting out of hand. One second he was dancing through fields, happily resigned, and now he was alone at the helm of that barge on the river, the rudder gone, fishtailing from bank to bank in the dark.

Run the *Slash* himself? In a week he'd be in prison for murdering Phoebe.

"Jennifer!" he yelled. She was running up the boardwalk and over the dune. "Jennifer!" Those maybe sniffles were definite sobs. She was ahead of him on the path, barely visible.

Jennifer was fast, but Adam was fast and desperate. He wasn't going to let her get away without straightening out this resignation mess. He caught her along the path but was so winded, he couldn't talk. "Wait . . . please . . ." He put up his finger and gulped for air.

She ran off again. Adam was pissed. Jennifer wasn't like this. *He* was like this. She was the responsible one. *He* was supposed to be running off. Adam had no intention of letting everything get switched around. She was going to get back to her responsible self and help him figure a way out of this.

A block from his street he caught up, but this time, he wasn't getting faked out. He dived, grabbed her knees, and executed a jolting tackle that knocked her off her feet. The two of them rolled, coming to rest against the dune, gasping for air.

For a while, they just lay there, catching their breath and gazing at the sky. Finally Adam said, "You're not running away again?"

"No," Jennifer said, and she was laughing. "It's hard running on two broken legs."

"I only did it because you deserved it."

They knew what they had to do. They had to write the story and say that the survey was a mistake and apologize. They had to print the best bully stories kids wrote on the ballots. They had to point out that an amazing number of kids got a least one vote — seventy-five altogether — meaning that bullying was more widespread than they'd ever thought and that a person who seemed like a bully to some might be a model human to others. (Adam was sure he was a perfect example of this.)

And then they had to do the hardest part. They had to go to Shadow before they told anyone about the results and give him fair warning. And Tish, too.

And finally — there was no way out — they had to print those stupid results.

It was good to have a plan and for a while they lay there, happily looking at the stars and discovering new constellations. "Those two stars," Adam said. "That's Orion tutoring Ursa Major for the state math test."

Jennifer squinted. "I see it," she said. "But are you sure it's math?"

"Absolutely," said Adam. "That star on the left — that's a calculator, plus a math review workbook and seven number-two pencils."

They laughed, but not enough. Orion's calculator reminded Adam about tabulating the bully results, and he got quiet again.

"Does church help?" he asked.

"Help?" said Jennifer. "Help what?"

"You know, having faith that things will turn out right?"

"You mean like the bully survey?" said Jennifer.

"Well, no. Well kind of, yeah. But just in general," said Adam. "I guess I wonder if I'm missing something. We don't go to church like you."

"So you're afraid God won't help you?" said Jennifer. "Is that why you won't let me resign? You think I'm better connected upstairs?"

Jennifer glanced Adam's way and caught a small smile, then quickly looked at the stars again. It was the only way to talk about this.

"You make it sound like a joke," he said. "I'm serious."

"I know," said Jennifer. "Do you believe in God?"

Adam took a while to answer. "I only see two explanations for this," he said, pointing at the spectacular night sky. "Either it's infinite—there's always been matter, always will be. Or God got it started. But here's the weird part I think about—

either way, you need faith. I mean, you can explain what infinite is—anyone can memorize Devillio's definition—but you can't really comprehend it. You can't get your brain around this thought that there's no beginning to the universe, that it's always been there. So I figure you get your pick: faith in infinity or faith in God."

"You didn't answer," she said. "Which one?"

"I don't know," said Adam. "At night I believe in God, or at least I pray. Especially when I'm full of worries. It's not like a real prayer. I don't know any real prayers. I just made up this thing thanking God for all the good stuff in my life and asking Him to look after me and my parents and my grandpa Harold, who died. And then, I just . . . well . . . ask for help for whatever mess I'm in."

"That last part," said Jennifer. "That must be the longest part of the prayer."

"You're a riot," said Adam.

"Sounds like a real prayer to me," she said softly.

"Anyway," Adam continued, "in the morning it feels like I have to get up and do it all by myself. I guess what I'm saying is since I mostly just pray at night when I'm scared and I'm asking for a favor and it's just a made-up prayer and I don't go to church—"

"Does it count?" said Jennifer.

"Yeah," Adam whispered.

"I think so," she said. "Our minister's always saying that prayer is not just for Sundays, that coming to church is no guarantee you'll get your name in the Good Book. He says it's how you treat people day to day, with kindness and stuff. I personally can't believe God would be so petty, like there was this one prayer everyone had to memorize and say every minute, or else they go to, you know, rhymes with *Taco Bell*. I've been to lots of churches and temples — there's definitely not one prayer. But it always feels the same: there's a power greater than us and we need help."

"I agree with that," said Adam.

"Actually," said Jennifer, "the proper response is, 'Amen, sister.'"

"I don't think I'm that advanced," said Adam.

"Tell me—" Jennifer began, but then screamed and so did Adam.

A blinding light was shining in their eyes. "WHAT'S GOING ON HERE, AS IF I DON'T KNOW?" bellowed a man's voice. Somewhere behind the voice was the crackling of a police radio. It took Adam's eyes a minute to adjust, and then he realized it was a flashlight. And the man shining it was wearing the official yellow all-seasons Windbreaker of a civic association security guard.

"Isn't this cute?" the man said. "My favorite soap opera, *Love in the Dunes.* Either of you live here in River Path? Or is this a pleasure trip?"

Adam explained he lived down the street.

"You better head home, son," the guard said. "You know you're not supposed to be in the dunes after dark."

Actually, Adam knew that was the kind of rule they made up when they couldn't think of anything you did wrong.

"You want to tell me what was going on?" the security guard said. "So's I can write my report. Or should I take a wild guess?"

"If you must know," said Jennifer, dusting off grass and sand, "we were talking about religion."

"Religion, oh that's good," the guard said. "I've caught lots of people in these dunes doing nooky-nooky, hanky-panky, and stinky-winky, but this is the first time anyone blamed religion."

chapter 18

The Science Unfair

Adam's dad dropped him off for the science fair a few minutes before seven A.M., the official set-up time. Already there was a long line of parents determined to get good display spots up front for their kids' projects.

When Eddie the janitor unlocked the gym door, Adam was nearly trampled. One parent speared him in the ribs with a poster board, and as Adam doubled over in pain, another jabbed him in the back with a fluorescent light. Then Adam made the mistake of going to the boys' room to see if he was bleeding. While he was gone, his project was moved to the far end of the table. "We needed an electric outlet for our project," a dad said. "Hope you don't mind."

Once the projects were set up, the day was spent waiting to be judged by a Harris teacher. All morning, Adam kept an eye on Devillio. The man was either on his cell or with some big-shot grown-up. Adam did not see him talk to a single kid until the *Citizen-Gazette-Herald-Advertiser* arrived. Then Devillio posed for the photographer in front of a bunch of test tubes, pretending to talk to students from the Big Four ethnic flavors.

Adam was judged after lunch. The man's name card said Mr. Buchanan. The only thing Adam knew about him was he coached lacrosse and looked it. He had a buzz cut and muscles that stuck out of his short-sleeved shirt, and he moved like a man who was used to knocking over people.

Adam tried sticking in as much grown-up language as possible as he explained his project, so everything would sound highly scientific. He talked about the constancy of the slope correlating adult support and student achievement. He described the clustering of results and how he'd calculated each cluster for both mean and average. He talked about the size of his survey sample and the margin of error.

Occasionally he glanced at Mr. Buchanan. The teacher seemed to be asleep standing up. The man kept saying, "I see," and "interesting," but Adam noticed that he wasn't saying them in the right places.

Mr. Buchanan was holding a stack of judging forms, each in triplicate; about half appeared to be filled out. Several had an *H* written on top, which Adam figured probably meant honors student.

The teacher picked up Adam's research paper and leafed through it in seconds, which either meant he was the fastest reader on earth or he was checking to make sure there were words on every page.

"So," he finally said, "what you're saying — when parents support children academically, the kids do better. Is that it?"

"Basically," said Adam.

"And the less parent support, the lower the academic performance?"

"Yes," said Adam.

"OK," said Mr. Buchanan. "I get it. Seems pretty sensible. Good job."

"Um," said Adam, "do you understand —"

"I got it," said Mr. Buchanan. "I particularly like

235

the margin of error analysis. That's real honors work. I've got to keep moving. Still have a bunch . . ."

"But—"

"Look," Mr. Buchanan said. "I'm only supposed to spend four minutes per project. It's not fair if you . . ."

The man was walking away, and Adam went hurrying after him. "Do you know what this is about?" Adam pleaded, waving his paper. "The science fair. The Harris science fair."

"Of course," said Mr. Buchanan. "It's all about the science fair and the glory of going on to the county fair. But you're not the only one who wants to win. Every honors student—"

"No!" said Adam. "My project is about *this* science fair. About kids getting help on projects for *this* science fair."

The teacher froze. He leaned forward until his face was right in Adam's. "This is about Harris parents doing their kids' projects?" he whispered.

Adam nodded.

"You're kidding."

The teacher grabbed Adam by the arm and dragged him back to his display. He studied the project board as if he'd never seen it before. He opened

Adam's report and actually read it. He kept saying, "unbelievable," "amazing," and this time, Adam noticed, he was saying it in the right places.

"This really will do well at the county fair," Mr. Buchanan said. "I could see it going to the states. I imagine it'll bring big changes around here. Mr. Devillio approved this?"

Adam nodded. "He checked the abstract. The only thing he said was change the font."

"Wonderful," said Mr. Buchanan. "I give Mr. Devillio credit. Most people in his position would not be so open-minded. Great job. I've never seen such an original project."

In the evening, the gym was open for the hour before the awards ceremony so family members could see the projects. Adam hated this part even more than the early morning setting-up riots. It was a zoo. There was so little time, and since every middle-school kid did a project, tons of family members showed up, clogging the center aisles.

Adam tried to see his friends' displays, including Jennifer's, but got exhausted battling the swirling masses and wandered over to the far aisles in the back of the gym. They were almost empty. A lot of the displays looked weak, and some weren't even real science projects—there was no experiment or hypothesis that was tested. Adam noticed a crooked coat-hanger atom with Styrofoam balls and a DNA double helix made from elbow macaroni that didn't stand up.

Two boys Adam recognized from gym class were going down the far aisle, joking loudly about how bad those projects were.

Adam's first impulse was to make a nasty crack, but then he got a better idea. He'd make the jerks famous. He pulled out a pen and the science fair program to use for taking notes.

"Excuse me," Adam said, "I'm doing a little story on the fair for the *Slash*. Mind if I ask a few questions?"

"Whoa, rad," said one. "We going to be on TV?"

"Almost," said Adam. He didn't have to ask their names. They wrote them down, they were so anxious to be quoted.

Adam explained he'd overheard them joking about the projects in the far aisle. He asked if they thought it was hard for kids who didn't get help from parents.

"Nah, they're just slack," said the boy. "They don't care."

"They blow it off," said the other. "They know they suck."

Adam nodded and wrote fast.

"You going to put that in the paper?" said one.

"Rad," said the other. "First time on MTV. I like it."

Adam thanked them and walked away. It would make a nice paragraph—the bad feelings caused by an unfair fair. He was making sure he could read the quotes when a grown-up he didn't know started talking to him.

"Every time I see you, you're making notes," she said.

It was a mom, and she looked familiar, but Adam couldn't place her.

"You don't remember?" she said. "You interviewed me at the board meeting a few months ago."

Outraged Single Mother! The one who was so angry about homework and parents doing kids' science projects.

What timing. Adam mentioned he'd tried phoning

her but when she never called back, he figured she was mad and gave up.

"No," she said. "Not mad. Just crazy busy. It's my fault. Raising three kids and a full-time job in the city—it's a lot. So what are you doing over here in science fair ghetto? You seem like a front-row center kid."

Adam explained about his own project and how he'd actually documented that kids who got the most help from their parents got the best scores. "I'm doing a news story on it, too," he said. "For the *Slash.*"

"Well, thank you," she said. "I've been saying that for years and no one will listen."

This was great; it wasn't often you got your whole story reported in one aisle. He asked if he could take notes.

"Are you kidding?" she said. "I wrote this all out in a letter to the superintendent. Be my guest."

"What did he say?" Adam asked.

"Oh, he bounced me down to some first deputy something or other, who bounced me to—I can't remember. I had a meeting with some Bleepin idiot."

"Dr. Bleepin?" said Adam. "A real kid person?"

"That's him," she said.

Outraged Single Mother told Bleepin that a science

fair was a wonderful thing, but the projects should be done in class, with help from teachers, so everyone had the same chance.

"My oldest is in college now," she told Adam, "and when she was at Harris, they did the projects in class. It worked well."

"Really?" said Adam. "Why'd they stop?"

"I don't know," she said. "Bleepin blamed the state testing." Dr. Bleepin told Outraged Single Mother that in the last ten years, the politicians had imposed state tests that dictated what teachers had to cover, practically paragraph by paragraph, cramming in so much to be memorized, there was no time to have kids do projects in school. "Bleepin said they had no choice; it was either do the projects at home or end the fair. What I do know?" she continued, gesturing around the gym. "This is not right. It is wrong to publicly humiliate children this way."

She led Adam along the back aisle, stopping in the far corner of the gym. "This is not for your article," she said. "Strictly off the charts." It was her son's project. It was supposed to show how an aquifer worked, and there was one part Adam found particularly smart. While an aquifer had to be pointing downhill for gravity to carry the water, the display showed how small sections could actually go uphill. The kid had used mathematical formulas to calculate the angle and distance a section could point uphill and still permit the aquifer to function.

His model, however, was shaky. The aquifer was made of toilet-paper rolls sliced in half, along with shower-curtain hooks held together by tinfoil, Scotch tape, and Play-Doh. In several spots, it was falling down.

"It's fine," she said. "I told him how proud I am. But he knows. Do you have any idea how that makes me feel as a mom? Like I failed. Like I couldn't give him what the center-aisle kids got. He sees it's not fair and that's a lesson you hate a kid to learn too early."

She turned away. Adam was getting this bad feeling that something personal and embarrassing was about to happen. But when Outraged Single Mother looked back, she was smiling. "You know the old saying," she said. "'Don't cry for me, Argentina.' You write that the news from the Harris science fair is not all bad. You tell your readers that life is no fifty-yard dash; it's a marathon. We lost this time, but there's a ways to go. As a mom, you pray this won't make them so angry they get bitter—just angry enough to get even."

Sitting in the auditorium, waiting for the awards, Adam felt like a million bucks. He'd pulled it off. Never had one of his investigations gone so smoothly. He'd come a long way since that day Devillio yelled at him. Adam had finished all his interviews, and they were on the record. His research had shown beyond a doubt that parents were doing the top projects. In a matter of minutes, he was going to win a top award. Even Mr. Buchanan had said that his was the most original project he'd ever seen. There were going to be big changes around here. Adam wasn't even worried about interviewing Devillio for the story. What's the worst the man could say? Claim he didn't know parents were helping? Big deal. Adam would print it. Readers would see the truth. An award-winning project says it all.

The ceremony was the same every year. Mr. Devillio welcomed everyone and introduced all the dignitaries, including school board members, the principal, and the Harris science teachers. Then he spoke on the illustrious history of the fair and the richly rewarding value of research.

It was nearly eight thirty when they were ready to announce the awards. There were two major groups. The first kids called to the stage were the silver medalists. These were the twenty-five who scored 90 to 94 on their projects.

They were to be followed by the gold medalists, who scored 95 and above and would go on to the county competition.

The only worry for a top student like Adam was if he had somehow messed up and gotten a 94 and so would win only a silver. Adam was sure that was not going to be a problem, but you could never be totally sure. He was a little tense until all twenty-five silver medalists had been announced and his name was not called.

He'd done it.

"And now," said Mr. Devillio, "the gold medalists. Everyone, of course, is a winner at the fair. You don't have to win a medal. Just taking part . . ."

Adam couldn't believe the way adults lied. How did they do it without blinking? They must spend hours practicing lies in front of the mirror.

As Adam waited, it occurred to him that he probably was the only one in the Top 25 who'd done the project himself. It was a proud feeling.

Adam's parents sat in the back, where most of the adults were. Adam was near the front with friends. As their names were called, the rest of the kids in the row leaned back in their chairs so the winners could squeeze by and hurry to the stage. Jennifer beamed when it was her turn, and she hurried past him and up the stage steps, shaking Devillio's hand and taking her gold medal. Adam was going to try not to smile. He didn't want to look too show-offy. Still, he didn't blame Jennifer; it was hard holding it in.

One by one they marched up. And then Mr. Devillio said, "A final round of applause for our gold medalists." There were hoots and whistles, and kids were stomping their feet.

"And that concludes the 32nd Annual Harris Middle School Science Fair. Thank you for coming. Have a safe trip home."

Parents and kids surged to the front of the auditorium, crowding up to congratulate the winners.

Adam sat in his seat, too shocked to move. He

was the only one still sitting in his row. This could not be. Something had gone wrong. His heart was pounding. It was impossible. Obviously they'd made a mistake. This was ridiculous. Come on. He knew what had happened. He jumped to his feet and pushed his way through the crowd.

As he neared the front, he spotted Jennifer, who'd come down from the stage. "What's going on?" she asked. "How could you not win? That's ridiculous."

"Yeah," said Adam, "I'm pretty sure I know what went wrong. I'm getting it straightened out."

He crowded past her to Devillio. There were so many important adults around the man that Adam had to wait a long time. Everyone had to tell Devillio what a great job he'd done again this year.

Finally, there was a break in the brownnosing, and Adam hurried over. "Mr. Devillio," Adam said, "I think there's been a mistake."

"A mistake?" said Mr. Devillio. "What kind of mistake?"

Adam said he was pretty sure he'd won an award and asked Mr. Devillio to please look, in case there was an oversight.

"I don't think so," said Mr. Devillio. "We had fifty medals and gave out fifty. But I'd be glad to check. What's your name?"

Adam told him and Mr. Devillio said, *"Canfield* with a *C* or *K?"* Mr. Devillio looked through the two sheets with the prize winners. "Don't see it," he said. "You can check yourself."

Adam tried to read the names, but could not make them out—his eyes were too blurry.

"Now, everyone does get a certificate of participation," Mr. Devillio said. "You'll get yours later this week. They're quite handsome. They have a raised blue seal . . ."

chapter 19

Pink Sheets

Adam had to find this Mr. Buchanan; it was his only chance. Something evil had happened between the time Mr. Buchanan judged the project in the afternoon and the awards ceremony at night, and though Adam didn't have a clue how it was done, he knew who had done it.

Adam had to give the Devil his due — if Devillio had left any fingerprints, Adam couldn't find them.

Before school, Adam slipped into the main office, checked the teacher mailboxes, and got Mr. Buchanan's room number. All morning between periods, he rushed to Mr. Buchanan's room but never got to the man.

Five times he tried and failed. Either Mr. Buchanan was in his room speaking to someone or he was in the hallway, hurrying people to class.

More than once, Adam was sure he'd seen a flicker of recognition on the teacher's face, but Mr. Buchanan did not give in to it.

Hunting Mr. Buchanan between periods was awful, and Adam was repeatedly late for class. Two teachers—Devillio was one—gave him detentions. (If Devillio had known the real reason, Adam was sure he would have had to serve those detentions in a maximum security prison.)

One more detention and Adam would get an in-school suspension. An entire day, sitting in a room, not permitted to go to class. He'd have to make up the work he missed, and worse, they'd call his parents. His mom and dad had been watching him like a hawk. He could tell they were worried that he hadn't won anything at the science fair. They didn't talk about it, but he knew they were scared the robbery had changed him.

And the harder he worked to straighten things out, the deeper he sank.

/////

At the end of lunch, Adam spotted Mr. Buchanan again. The teacher was leaning against a wall, eating an apple, and joking with boys from the lacrosse team. Adam dumped his lunch and hurried along the back wall so Mr. Buchanan wouldn't see him approach. He waited for the bell so there'd be plenty of commotion to cover him. As kids rose to leave, Adam stepped into the teacher's path. "How you doing, Mr. Buchanan?" Adam said. "Can we talk for a minute?"

Mr. Buchanan leaned forward so close, Adam could see every hair in his buzz cut. The teacher was chomping his apple and smiling between chews. "Listen good," he said in a barely audible voice. "Don't approach me again. Every time I turn around, you're watching me. Stalking a teacher is a serious offense. I'd hate to have to report you to my department chairman." Then Mr. Buchanan straightened up and in a loud voice called out to no one in particular, "Have a nice day."

How could Adam prove it without Mr. Buchanan? But then, for all Adam knew, this guy Buchanan was Devillio's best buddy. Or worse, maybe, Devillio was his uncle. Adam never could tell what was holding adults together.

He figured that Mr. Buchanan had been excited about the project, then talked to Devillio and was ordered to change the grade.

Adam knew he should tell Jennifer. But he didn't have the energy to lay out the whole tangled affair. He hated people who whined about their grades. When kids told him they deserved a better mark, Adam nodded. But what he really thought was they should try harder and bellyache less.

That afternoon, Jennifer asked if he'd taken care of his science fair score, and all he said was, "Working on it."

Adam served one of the detentions after school, which made him late for baseball practice. Each piece of trouble led to more troubles. The coach wouldn't be interested in excuses; he wasn't the type. Adam would have to do laps around the field.

The locker room was empty, always a creepy feeling. When the place was full of kids, there was so much talk, that's all he thought about. Alone, he realized what a drippy, stinky place it was. He laced his cleats, pulled on his hooded sweatshirt and baseball cap (frontward—he didn't need any more problems), then grabbed his glove and walked out to the field.

It was drizzling and cold. Adam needed to break a sweat and started jogging. If at that moment he could have any wish, he'd wish to be home, in bed, taking a nap. Bad news wore him out.

He passed the tennis courts and was thankful that the fence was covered with a green mesh; the last thing he needed was one of Jennifer's cheery, yoohooey-Louie, wavey hellos.

The girls' softball team was scrimmaging on the near diamond.

The boys' team was those dots on the far diamond.

And then Adam felt it, the voice. He felt it before he heard the words, the breath warm on the back of his neck. "Keep running," the voice said. "Don't turn around. I'll say this once. You can come to my room at exactly 2:55 tomorrow. I won't be there. You have exactly ten minutes. If I come back and anything is missing—if one paper is out of place—I will notify my department chairman. If I come back and there is a student in my room, I will detain the unauthorized student and notify my chairman."

That was it. He hurried past Adam, picking up steam as he raced toward the lacrosse team on the far field. Then he raised his stick and in a voice as loud and shocking as a plane hidden by the clouds breaking the sound barrier, he boomed, "YOU SCREW UP AND YOU'RE DEAD!"

Adam saw all the lacrosse dots on the far field lift their tiny sticks and heard them roar back, "KILL!"

The next twenty-four hours dragged unbearably. Adam worried that it might be a trap. He feared he'd be searching the room and Buchanan and Devillio would burst in, accompanied by security guards armed with Palm Pilots flashing Adam's picture.

Maybe he should give up. If he went there at 2:55, he'd miss serving his detention, which would earn him a third detention. And an in-school suspension. And a call to his parents.

It might be time to admit defeat. He'd tried. It wasn't his job to save the human race. Everyone seemed to agree that it was an unfair world. Outraged Single Mother. Mr. Johnny Stack. Danny. All those great authors Erik Forrest knew who drank themselves into a stupor writing bad movies.

He wanted to quit, go home, sleep.

But he couldn't.

He could not let the Devil get away with it.

He found his running-club watch in the top drawer buried among his boxers and socks. At breakfast, as his dad listened to NPR, Adam set the watch to the radio time so it would be exact.

As usual, his dad had a bad case of nose trouble. "What's going on?" he asked. "A watch? We having our annual spring punctuality drive?"

"Very funny, Dad," said Adam. "You're a riot."

"Adam, seriously," said his dad. "You're not having late problems again, are you?"

"Oh no, Dad," said Adam. "No way. As a percentage of my problems, late problems are way down there. I'd estimate less than two percent of my gross national problems."

He grabbed his lunch, kissed his dad, and hurried to catch the bus before his father got to the follow-up questions.

/////

The moment he entered the room, he planned to activate the stopwatch option for ten minutes.

The door was closed, the shade drawn, but when he turned the handle, it opened. He stepped in and eased the door shut.

Now what? He did not know what he was looking for but was hoping it would be obvious. He glanced around. Nothing stuck out. He looked at the front board. It appeared to be a normal lesson on genetics. He thought of crazy stuff—like the first letter of each line might be a secret code. But even mixing up letters, he couldn't think of anything that *MGDHHPL* spelled.

The computer was off. The tables where students sat were empty, except one on the far side by the windows; a notebook was leaning against the gas jet. He hurried over, but it was just some kid's lab book.

In the front behind Mr. Buchanan's desk were two filing cabinets. He figured he'd start with *S* for science fair. But when he tugged, the drawers were all locked, except the bottom ones, which were full of lacrosse balls and duct tape.

He glanced at his watch. What an idiot! He'd

forgotten to set the stopwatch option. Some behaved with grace under pressure; Adam got stupid. It was 2:56, so he set the stopwatch for nine minutes, but when he flicked back, the time said 2:57. Idiot! The stopwatch wasn't exactly coordinated with the time.

He checked the top of Mr. Buchanan's desk. In the center was a binder of lesson plans that he flipped through quickly. There was a file of notices from the main office, a file for lockdown procedures, a file of lab safety guidelines, a file of takeout restaurant menus, a file of the middle-school sports team schedules.

There was a file of photos, including one of Mr. Buchanan and Ms. Lummus, a pretty English teacher, which would have made a nice item if the *Slash* had a gossip column.

There was another photo of the science department staff that made Adam's eyes bug out. Someone had drawn horns and a pointed tail on Mr. Devillio.

This was hopeful, but it made Adam even more desperate to find whatever he was looking for.

The stopwatch option said 7:58 left.

It wasn't exact.

He was going through stuff on top of the desk

with one hand and trying desk drawers with the other. The middle one was locked, as were all three on the left.

So he wasn't looking down when he felt the bottom right drawer respond to his tug. He expected to see mouthpieces and jockstraps—this Mr. Buchanan definitely was no Gregor Mendel. But to Adam's surprise, there was a stack of manila folders.

Please be it, he said to himself before yanking out a folder.

It said SCIENCE FAIR JUDGING. Adam's heart was pounding. Inside were all Mr. Buchanan's pink sheets, the triplicate forms judges saved for their records. They weren't alphabetical, and Adam frantically searched, finding his form near the bottom.

His eyes raced down the scoring sheet.

The rubric had over a dozen categories to be graded: abstract, summation, poster display, originality, verbal presentation, research technique. All Adam's scores were 70s. He strained to see if any of those 70s might have started as 90s, but they hadn't.

Rifling through the sheets, he noticed the aquifer project.

The kid got an 82, better than Adam.

That was it. This was too crazy. He had to get out of there. He closed the folder and put it back in the drawer.

That's when he noticed. There was a second folder, a skinny one. He could see pink inside, and when he opened it, there was one score sheet.

Adam's.

Every score was high 90s.

The final grade was 98.

He knew it. He knew it!

The stopwatch option said 4:48 left.

It wasn't exact.

He grabbed the two pink sheets and raced for the door. He had to find a copy machine. Where? The main office! Too many people, too many questions. The *Slash* copy machine? No one had refilled the toner for months. Adam had tried to make that Phoebe's job. He'd explained to Phoebe that because she was a cub reporter, to earn a place on the staff, certain menial jobs were expected of her.

Phoebe had called Adam a blatant sexist and stomped out, and nobody had refilled the toner since November.

Never in his life had Adam so desperately needed

a copy machine. Mr. Brooks! His world history teacher. Mr. Brooks loved Adam. He had stood by Adam during the Marris investigation. He was the social studies chairman. He'd let Adam use the department copy machine in a second.

Adam raced to Mr. Brooks's room, stopping in the doorway to catch his breath.

The stopwatch option said 3:21 left.

It wasn't exact.

Mr. Brooks was at his desk, correcting papers. Adam loved this man. Even sitting alone after school, his suit coat was buttoned. And he was writing comments in the margins; no rubrics for Mr. Brooks.

Mr. Brooks looked up, smiled, and welcomed Adam in his favorite dead language. *"Salve, amicus!"*

Adam quickly explained that he needed a huge favor fast and asked to use the copy machine.

"Salve, amicus," Mr. Brooks repeated.

"Salve, amicus," Adam mumbled. "Please, Mr. Brooks."

"It's not anything . . . you know . . . ?"

"Nothing dirty," said Adam. "I swear. It's for the *Slash.* Please, Mr. Brooks, I'm on a tight deadline."

"Tight deadline?" said Mr. Brooks. "Isn't the *Slash* a monthly?" He got up, and they headed to the social studies office down the hall. Adam knew it had to be his imagination, but Mr. Brooks seemed to be taking baby steps. "Please hurry," Adam said.

"Festina lente," said Mr. Brooks. "Haste makes waste."

"He who hesitates is lost," said Adam.

"Maxima enim, patientia virtus," said Mr. Brooks. "Patience is a virtue."

"A rolling stone gathers no moss," said Adam.

"Oh, Adam," said Mr. Brooks. *"Non uno die Roma aedificata est*—Rome wasn't built in a day." He lay the first pink sheet on the glass, pulled down the cover, and pressed PRINT.

A yellow light flashed. "Out of 8½-by-11 paper," said Mr. Brooks. "It'll take a minute to replace."

"Please, Mr. Brooks," said Adam, "can't we just use 8½-by-14 legal size?"

"Adam, I'm surprised," said Mr. Brooks. "Such a waste of trees. I thought from the story on the three-hundred-year-old tree that the *Slash* was pro-tree."

"Mr. Brooks, remember you taught us about Magellan and how he had to go to that dopey teenage king and beg him for a fleet of boats to go around the world?"

"Very good, Adam. King Charles I of Spain."

"Remember you told us how desperate Magellan was to restore his good name after his troubles in Morocco and how he'd do anything to get his reputation back? Well, I'm begging you, Mr. Brooks. Give me the boats. I need the boats!"

"All right," said Mr. Brooks. "I get the message. Two 8½-by-14 boats coming up."

Adam grabbed the copies, shouted his thanks, then raced back to Mr. Buchanan's room.

The stopwatch option said 53 seconds.

It wasn't exact.

He raced to Mr Buchanan's desk, opened the bottom drawer, put the pink sheets back, closed the drawer, and raced to the door.

The stopwatch option said 28 seconds.

It wasn't exact.

A miracle—he'd done it.

And then he heard Mr. Buchanan's voice in the hallway; the teacher was talking to someone. Devillio?

The stopwatch option said 20 seconds.

Why wasn't it exact?

Adam frantically looked around the room. He could hide under a table. That was stupid. There was a supply closet in back, but if the door was locked, he'd be done; they'd be in the room. The buzzer on his stopwatch sounded.

The knob was turning.

He hopped on top of the built-in bookcases that lined the far wall. He lay flat. And then he rolled out the window.

chapter 20

Copy Power

The phone rang at seven thirty the next morning as they rushed to get ready for work and school. With a call that early, Adam's parents feared someone was ill.

Adam feared the call would make him ill.

His mother took it, and Adam could tell she definitely had not won the Publishers Sweepstakes grand prize.

"We are breaking new ground," she said, hanging up. "That was the dean of discipline. Seems you're in big trouble, young man. One of us has to go with you to get you back into school. Adam, this is unbelievable. Were you going to say anything?"

Adam was trying to think fast. He didn't want to say a word until he found out what they had on him. There were lots of possibilites. Fortunately, he was catching a cold. He pulled out a handkerchief and blew his nose hard. Maybe it'd generate some sympathy.

Right.

"Suspended!" yelled his mother. "You, Adam Canfield. Honors student. Four-pluser. Don't you have anything to say? Aren't you sorry?"

Adam was delighted to be sorry; he just needed to know exactly what to be sorry for. He hated manipulating his parents but had no choice. He dropped to one knee, lifted his arms high, and hollered, "What did I do? I didn't do anything. Just tell me one single thing I did."

"What did you do?" yelled his mother. "Where do I begin? You failed to show up for detention, not that you felt you should tell us you even had a detention. Two detentions, no less. So now it's strike three! Let me shake your hand. Please, stand to accept the award. You've won a day of in-school suspension. What's going on? You bomb at the science fair, but you're number one with the Dean of Discipline?"

Adam felt enormous relief. That was all? He'd done it! He pumped his fist.

The moment he did, he knew it was a mistake.

"You're celebrating?" It was his father's turn. "Do you know what they call someone who does something wrong and feels no remorse? A sociopath! You know what happens to sociopaths? They grow up to be serial killers. They murder innocent people and sit in the courtroom smirking."

"No, Dad, I swear, I'm sorry. I wasn't happy about getting in trouble. I was just afraid it was something worse."

"Worse?" said his father. "There's something worse? Adam, we're on the slippery slope. No science fair medal. Suspended from school. I notice your hair's getting a little long. Half the time, your baseball cap's on backward. What's next?"

Adam dropped his head. He tried to look like a person who would never smirk in a courtroom.

He blew his nose.

It might have worked. His parents left the room and were whispering.

When they returned, they started by saying that they knew he was a good boy and was under a lot of pressure.

Then they said they were worried he might have been traumatized by being mugged and felt it would be good for him to see a therapist. They kept emphasizing that his problems seemed to have started after the mugging. "It doesn't mean we think you're crazy," said his father. "It just means it might be good if you talked things out with someone. Even this cold you have. Emotional problems can lead to physical illness."

Adam considered protesting. The only reason he had a cold was that his baseball coach believed in practicing in level-five hurricanes.

But Adam held his tongue. Things were going too good. All he said was "OK."

When his dad went to get the car keys, Adam sat back and let out his breath. He'd pulled it off. It was the second terrific thing that happened to him in twenty-four hours.

The night before, he'd lain in bed and thanked God for putting Mr. Buchanan's room on the first floor.

Jennifer and Phoebe walked into 306, looked at each other, dropped their backpacks, executed synchronized swoons, and fell to the floor, apparently dead.

"Very funny," said Adam, who was finishing

putting toner in the *Slash* copy machine. "You guys are hilarious. I assume you know that slapstick is *the* lowest form of humor."

Phoebe lifted her head. "The pun is the lowest form of humor," she said, and flopped back to a dead position.

"You two can stay dead the rest of your lives for all I care," said Adam. "I will never enter a room again without knowing the location of the nearest copy machine." He took out the two science fair score sheets and made copies. "Too bad you're dead," he said. "These may be the most important documents ever to enter this room."

Immediately Phoebe jumped to her feet. "The Top Ten Bully list!" she shouted. "Let me see."

"Get back," said Adam. "I liked you better when you were dead."

Jennifer was still on the floor but now was glaring at the ceiling. "Phoebe!" she said. "I told you the coeditors had things to do before showing you the list. I told you we were afraid the list would hurt some good people. Is any of this familiar?"

"Yeah," said Phoebe. "But I thought maybe the junior coeditor was finished."

"I just told you on the way up," said Jennifer. "Ten seconds ago."

"I see your point," said Phoebe.

The three gathered at the newsroom conference table—a picnic bench that some editor years ago had saved from the trash. "So here's the good news," said Jennifer. "The public meeting on the three-hundred-year-old tree was great, plus Phoebe dug up amazing stuff from her secret iceberger sources."

Phoebe was beaming shamelessly.

"It's nice to see you happy," Jennifer said. "Tell the junior coeditor what you got."

"Quite a story," Phoebe said. "But to appreciate it, you have to go back to ancient Mesopotamia . . ."

Adam shot Jennifer a panicked look.

"Phoebe, we're in a hurry," said Jennifer. "How about if I tell Adam how you nailed it for the front page?"

"Front page?" said Phoebe. She leaped up and started sashaying her hips and snapping her fingers in the latest version of her renowned front-page dance. "The streak goes on!"

Jennifer motioned for quiet. She explained that to determine the sturdiness of the climbing tree, the state forestry department took borings of the trunk and discovered that the tree is a shell with a two-foot hollow center shaft surrounded by an outer ring of solid wood one foot wide that supports the tree.

"Sounds like it might fall any second," said Adam.

"Exactly my reaction," Jennifer said.

"This is the front-page part," said Phoebe. "The streak goes on!"

It was nowhere near that bad. After reading Phoebe's first story in the *Slash,* a secret source mailed her an inspection report of the tree that was done twenty years ago by the Tremble Nature Center. That old study calculated that the climbing tree had a two-foot hollow shaft and a solid outer ring one foot wide. "In other words," said Jennifer, "the tree is exactly as strong today as twenty years ago. Nothing changed!"

"And for those twenty years," said Phoebe, "it never fell once. Baby, the streak goes on."

Adam was impressed, but Phoebe made it hard to say so.

"It's a bit more complicated," said Jennifer.

"I'm really not sure we need this next part," said Phoebe. "It just slows down the story."

"Fairness," said Jennifer, "remember? The golden rule of journalism? Give both sides of the story."

At the public meeting, a forester told the audience about the 1802 copper beech tree at West Point Military Academy. In August 1989, experts finished an inspection, pronounced the tree hardy, and predicted it could live another hundred years.

"The next day," said Jennifer, "the trunk split in half. All that's left is a desk."

"Whoa," said Adam.

"So even though Phoebe's iceberg reporting has probably saved the climbing tree," said Jennifer, "we have to make clear that when it comes to old trees . . ."

"No guarantees," said Adam.

"I'm still not sure we need that last part," said Phoebe.

After Phoebe left, the coeditors discussed the Willows story, which was nearly done. They loved the way one source led them to the next source, one story to the next story.

Adam's visit to the Willows last fall for the story about Miss Bloch's gift to Harris led them to Mrs. Willard.

And Mrs. Willard led them to Pine Street Church.

And that led them to Reverend Shorty, who helped them on the Dr. King story.

And the Dr. King story gave Reverend Shorty confidence to trust them for the story about the Bolands buying up the Willows.

This time, Reverend Shorty gave Jennifer several juicy quotes *on the record.*

"If they keep boarding up homes," he said, "pretty soon there will be no houses left in Tremble that average working people can afford."

And: "Many children now attending Harris Elementary/Middle will be forced to move away."

They had just two things to do. They still had to interview kids from the Willows. Reverend Shorty gave Jennifer names of several families, plus there was Tish. Jennifer asked Adam to interview him; she said she'd feel funny doing it, after she and Tish had talked about it as friends.

"Friends?" said Adam.

"Just friends," said Jennifer.

"OK," said Adam.

Last and worst, Mrs. Boland had to be interviewed. "I dread that," Jennifer said. "I felt like she held us prisoner in our own newsroom."

"Don't worry," said Adam. "I've got a secret

plan. She won't trap us again. I dreamed about it."
Adam blew his nose.

"What secret plan?" asked Jennifer.

"You're looking at it," said Adam, blowing his
nose again. But that was all Jennifer got out of him.

He did, however, have lots to say about his science
fair investigation, and after swearing Jennifer to top
secrecy, told the whole story of the visit to Mr.
Buchanan's room.

Then he explained how he was going to fix his
science fair grade. He would go to Devillio and con-
front the man with the two score sheets. He wanted
to see Devillio beg for forgiveness. And if Devillio
dared rip up the evidence, Adam would flash two
fresh copies right in his pathetic face. "He'll never
forget my name again," said Adam.

"No offense," said Jennifer. "That's a rotten
plan." She accused Adam of letting "blood lust for
sweet revenge" cloud his judgment. She said that
if Adam went to him first, it would give Devillio
the chance to twist things around and blame Mr.
Buchanan. She said that Devillio would probably
run to the principal and act like he deserved credit

for uncovering this terrible plot. Then Devillio would look like the hero and Mr. Buchanan would get fired.

Jennifer believed that Adam's best hope was Mrs. Quigley. He needed to show her the two sets of science fair grades, explain his project, and then tell her what Devillio did.

"You think I can trust Mrs. Quigley?" Adam said. "Remember how she left us trapped in 306 with Mrs. Boland?"

"Remember how she gave us cookies and told us her dad was a newspaperman?" said Jennifer.

"Remember how nice the witch was in the first half of *Hansel and Gretel*?" said Adam. "And remember the oven in the second half?"

Jennifer tore a page from her notebook. On one side she wrote Mr. Devillio's name, on the other Mrs. Quigley's. "OK," she said. "Let's put down all the positive reasons for going to Devillio first."

Adam thought about it. He tapped his forehead to loosen up his brain juices.

All he could think of was blood lust for sweet revenge.

/////

The next morning, Adam stopped in the office and told Mrs. Rose he needed to see the principal. "It's important," he said, waving a sealed envelope marked CONFIDENTIAL.

Mrs. Rose said the principal was busy, but he could leave the envelope.

Adam hesitated.

"Don't worry, Adam," said Mrs. Rose, smiling kindly. "I won't lose it."

"It's not that," said Adam. "I made fifty copies of everything."

"Then we'll be fine," said Mrs. Rose. "Normally, the most we ever lose is twenty or thirty copies."

chapter 21

Ignore the Fools

"Want to see my Roger Clemens rookie card?" Shadow said. "No one can touch it except me. Nearly mint condition."

Jennifer nodded. This was the eighth time she'd seen it since Shadow joined the *Slash*. He held Roger up to her face. Jennifer liked looking at the card. It made Shadow happy.

She was dreading what she had to say. She figured that every day Shadow got treated ten times more unfairly than most kids. Now it was her turn. Her great bully survey.

"Roger Clemens must be your favorite," said Shadow. "You're really looking a lot. Mr. Johnny

Stack says, 'Don't let anyone near that card too long—it might disappear.'"

"I'm sorry," said Jennifer. "I was kind of lost in thought. Was that too long?"

"It was," said Shadow. "Forty-five seconds. Mr. Johnny Stack says, 'Anything more than thirty seconds is getting to be a lot.' You want to see my watch? It has the date, too. There's no time limit for seeing my watch."

Jennifer shook her head. "What I want to do," said Jennifer, "is apologize."

"Apologize?" Shadow looked surprised. Finally he said, "Did you not listen to a good person who was trying to tell you something important?"

Jennifer was lost.

"That's why Adam apologized," said Shadow.

"No, that's not it," said Jennifer.

Shadow took a deep sniff. "I don't smell a fart."

Jennifer burst out laughing. "Shadow," she said, touching his arm. "That's bad manners."

"No," said Shadow. "It's bad manners to fart in public," and he took another sniff. "It's not bad manners not to fart. You're OK as far as I can tell."

"Not totally OK," said Jennifer. Slowly, she led up to the bad news, telling him how they had assumed the bully list would be full of mean kids who deserved to be shamed, how she and Adam had felt sick after they counted the votes, and how they decided they couldn't kill the story, though they wanted to.

Shadow nodded, saying nothing.

"Some kids treated the survey like a goof," Jennifer continued. "They voted for people who should not be on the list because—I don't know— they're jerks and bullies themselves. They used the secret ballot to be mean."

He kept nodding. Did Shadow have a clue what she was talking about? "Are you following me?" she asked.

He nodded again.

"And one of the kids they did this to was you. You shouldn't be, but you're a top ten bully."

She was bracing herself, but he just kept looking at her. "Say something. Please."

"You're not mad at me?" said Shadow. "I checked 162 kids voting and that bossy, short girl—"

"Phoebe," said Jennifer.

"That bossy one did 161. But she would do 162, too, except there was no more one to do. So it couldn't be 161 + 1, 162, same as me. It was 161 + 0. Is that why you're mad?"

"Oh, Shadow, I'm not mad at you—I'm mad at

me," said Jennifer. "I'm mad at the idiots who saw you and wrote your name for a joke."

He was quiet, then said, "So many people know me. Before, only 107A knew. Now all them know me."

"That's not how you want to be known," said Jennifer. "It's not fair or true." She hesitated. "A lot of those kids voted for you just because you are 107A."

Shadow nodded. "Mr. Johnny Stack says there's a lot of anti-dismental people. He says, 'Theodore, just go about your business and ignore the fools and you'll be fine.' So, that's what I do. Ignore the fools and I'll be fine."

"Ignore the fools," repeated Jennifer. "We should make that the official *Slash* motto. And you know what? The kids in 306, we know how great you are."

"Yup," said Shadow, "a lot of people know me these days."

Jennifer wanted to shout with joy. She asked if she could give Shadow a hug.

"Nope," he said.

"Oh, come on," said Jennifer, stretching her arms toward him.

Shadow backed off. "No hugs," he said, gazing down. "I do not like hugs."

"How about a handshake?" asked Jennifer. "That OK?"

"That would be OK," he said.

Jennifer extended her hand, and Shadow gave her a firm, forthright handshake, just like he'd learned in his life skills class.

Adam's talk with Tish did not go nearly so well. Tish and his buddies were at their lunch table, and Adam asked to talk to him alone. They walked over to an empty spot along the wall.

"Ain't basketball season," said Tish. "Since when you looking for me out of season?"

"Right," said Adam. "Like you're calling me every minute to hang out."

"No biggy," said Tish. "Just saying. Seems a little questionable."

"This isn't why," said Adam, "but I've got to tell you something I should've said a long time ago." He thanked Tish for that day at the courts. "No joke," said Adam. "That big kid would have walked off with my ball. Or beat the crap out of me."

"No prob," said Tish. "I didn't do nothing. Just a

mix-up. That boy didn't know he was messing with the best *white* point guard at Harris."

"Very funny," said Adam. "You wait, my growth spurt's coming."

"I'm worried," said Tish, smiling.

"I can tell," said Adam.

Adam said there were two things he needed to talk about. He told Tish how the *Slash* was going to write about the Bolands and try to save the Willows. He told Tish they wanted to show that Willows kids who go to Harris could be forced to move away.

Adam asked if he could interview Tish.

Adam figured this would soften up Tish before talking about that stupid bully survey. Adam was sure Tish would appreciate it.

Big mistake.

Tish said he didn't want anyone knowing his private business, including where he lived. He said he didn't need to be saved, didn't need people feeling sorry for "poor Willows children," and he could take care of himself fine. "What you write in your paper don't have nothing to do with me," he said.

Adam stood there, mute.

"You said two things," Tish went on. "Come on, I got to be going. I don't got time for this pretend crap."

It was hard for Adam to tell Tish about the bully survey fast and include all the apologizing he'd planned to do.

Tish cut him off way before the end.

"How many black boys on that list?" Tish said. "There any whites?"

Adam explained that the top vote-getter was white.

"That kid's an animal," said Tish. "He'd be in juvey lockup, except who his parents are. I'm on a list with him?" He grabbed Adam by the shirt and pulled him close. "You make me puke," Tish said. "You don't know nothing about me. You don't know how I live."

A lunch aide hurried over. "Gentlemen, are we having a problem?" she asked.

"Yeah," said Tish. "I'm bullying this poor boy." He thrust out his hands. "Cuff me. I'll go peaceful."

"There's no problem," said Adam. "Just joking around. Ha, ha."

The aide gave them a hard look. "I'm watching," she said.

Tish leaned toward Adam. "You go write your hero stories. Big Adam going to save the Willows. Read all about it. Can't get his own basketball back hisself, but he's saving us. Just keep me out of it. And next time, get your own ball back, junior cheese."

Adam felt awful. He was in a daze when he heard his name over the loudspeaker in math, summoning him to the office.

Mrs. Rose led him in and offered him milk and two Moisty Deluxe. "Anything else I can get you, sweetie?" she said. "Mrs. Quigley will be right in."

It was amazing. When that evil Marris was principal, Mrs. Rose was known as the ominous Head. Now, working for Mrs. Quigley, she was the sugarplum fairy.

Adam hoped it was a good omen. But when Mrs. Quigley walked in, she didn't look sugary or plummy — she looked mad.

"I've never seen anything like this," she said.

Adam's heart sank. Danny was right: Beware of principals bearing cookies.

"Young man, I've been a principal twenty-five years in four schools, and NEVER have I seen such devious behavior. I am too old for this." She yanked open a drawer, grabbed Adam's confidential envelope, and shook the contents onto her desk.

"How did you get these score sheets?" she asked. "Students aren't given copies of their raw scores."

Adam hung his head.

"Now listen," she said. "This may be the most important question you answer in your middle-school life: Did you take these score sheets without permission?"

Adam was looking down. "No," he said.

"Did you break into Mr. Devillio's files to get these?"

"No," he said.

"Did you break into a classroom?"

"No."

"A window?"

Adam looked at Mrs. Quigley. Did she know? She was eyeing him real close. Maybe it was his imagination, but she didn't seem *that* worked up. Her face wasn't purple.

"A window," she repeated. "Did you climb in a window, young man?"

Climb *in* a window? "No!" Adam said cheerfully. "I definitely did not climb *in* any windows. If there's one thing that is one hundred percent guaranteed, I did not climb *in* a window. If you need me to swear on my grandpa Harold's holy grave—"

"I get it," she interrupted. "Did someone hand you these score sheets?"

"No," Adam said.

"Once more. How did you get them?"

Adam didn't know what to say. He couldn't give up Mr. Buchanan. Reporters had to protect their sources. Otherwise, no one would ever tell a reporter a secret again. What was he supposed to do?

He could not lie, and that wasn't because he was such a moral human.

He couldn't think of any believable lies fast enough that would stick.

"For the last time. How did you get those score sheets?"

"Please, Mrs. Quigley," said Adam. "A reporter can't give up his secret sources. I'm sorry."

Mrs. Quigley eyed him. "Secret sources," she said. "I suppose next thing, you'll be claiming protection under the First Amendment."

Adam's mind was racing. He needed all the protection he could get, but which amendment was that? He wished Jennifer was there. She had a great mind for remembering amendments. Every year, without fail, Adam did terribly on the U.S. Constitution unit. The teachers always talked about what an immortal document it was, and Adam had no doubt it would outlive him, but the words were so old-fashioned and general. The only amendment he could ever remember was the second, the right to bear arms. Guns! He could have used that amendment — he would have shot himself in the foot to distract Mrs. Quigley.

"I guarantee you," she said, "I won't be the last to ask you those questions. And I must say, you did fine. If you can keep this between us," she said, "I'm just as happy not knowing how you got the goods." She picked up the plate. "Another Moisty Deluxe?"

It took Adam several moments to realize what was happening, and then it all came flooding in and welling up. Jennifer was right. Mrs. Quigley was a force for good. Decency was not dead on the planet.

However, the cookies were not the only moisty thing in the room. Adam grabbed his handkerchief, gave a big blow and in the same motion, wiped those wet spots off his cheeks.

"Seems like everyone has a cold," Mrs. Quigley said, smiling. "Must be the change of weather."

Adam nodded; it was unbelievable how much the weather and everything else was changing. There was so much he wanted to say — he felt like giving this dear old acting principal the hug of the century. But he was so worked up, he couldn't move a muscle, not even his lip muscles.

Lucky for Adam, he didn't have to. Good reporters know when to keep their big mouths shut, and this was Adam's opportunity. Mrs. Quigley had a plan.

"It isn't perfect," she said. "But in real life, we have to compromise. If the world were fair, the devil would get his due."

Adam's eyes bugged out. *The Devil get his due?* Mrs. Quigley knew, too?

"For the purposes of this conversation," she said, "that's *devil getting his due* with a small *d.*"

She said that after a long talk with Mr. Devillio, plus an in-depth review of certain documents, the science chairman now realized that there had been an "unfortunate mistabulation," compounded by a "bureaucratic snafu" that had "impacted negatively, situationally speaking" on Adam's project.

Adam's score was 98, not 76.

The science chairman, of course, felt terrible. And as a result, he now saw Adam's project in a new light, Mrs. Quigley reported.

Mr. Devillio now realized it was entirely possible that parents were doing too much.

"He did mention," said Mrs. Quigley, "that just a few months ago he asked your class if parents were helping and everyone said no, including you."

"Wait," said Adam. "That's not fair—"

"You wait," said Mrs. Quigley. "I can envision what hearty give-and-take discussions Mr. Devillio encourages with his students."

Mrs. Quigley wasn't done. "Mr. Devillio and I agreed that the rescoring of your project did not need to be included in your news story. We agreed we could classify that as a private, teacher-student matter. I told him I didn't think there'd be a problem leaving that out of the story. Was I right?"

Adam didn't know what to say. He was so happy and couldn't care less, as long as the score was fixed. But he was nervous he might be breaking some journalism tenets.

"We can still write about parents doing the projects?" he asked.

"Oh yes," said Mrs. Quigley. "And you can include a comment from the acting principal that she intends to form a committee to see whether projects can be done during school in order to create a more fair fair. Would there be room for a quote like that?"

"Well . . . sure," said Adam. "Probably on the top of page one."

"I think if you talk to Mr. Devillio, you'll find he, too, supports this committee. And you'll see how shocked and saddened he was to learn that parents were doing projects."

"Shocked and saddened," repeated Adam.

"Shocked and saddened," said Mrs. Quigley. "So, that about does it for the science fair?"

When Adam nodded, she said, "One other thing. I saw you were on the list for in-school suspension. Would that by any chance have anything to do with this?"

"It might," said Adam.

"Do I want to know the details?" Mrs. Quigley asked.

"Nope," said Adam. "Don't think you do."

"Didn't think so," said Mrs. Quigley. "We'll just sentence you to time served. Come on. I'll walk you out." As they headed to the main office, Mrs. Quigley asked how the bully survey turned out.

"Bad," said Adam, filling her in on the problems

with the vote and their worries about printing the names.

Mrs. Quigley listened carefully. Adam loved that. She seemed like the kind of near-extinct adult who actually heard what kids said.

"I blame myself," she said when he'd finished. "I never should have allowed you to single out kids like that. I was thinking too much like a newspaperman's daughter. Not enough like a principal. I figured a bully story might give us the chance to bring in some professionals to work with students on the problem. Pinpoint kids who needed help. What are we going to do, Adam?"

Adam was tempted to suggest that Mrs. Quigley might kill the story. Boy, would that let him and Jennifer off the hook.

But he didn't think that was something a coeditor should suggest.

"I can't just kill it," she said. "That sends a bad message. Think. Wait — you did say seventy-five kids got at least one vote?" Mrs. Quigley slapped her hand on the counter. "I've got it!"

Everyone in the office looked up.

"Oops," said Mrs. Quigley. "Sorry. Don't mind

me." She motioned for Adam to come close and whispered in his ear.

Adam's face brightened. "Not bad for a grown-up idea," he said.

"Not bad at all," said Mrs. Quigley. "Can you keep another secret?"

Adam nodded, but this time, Mrs. Quigley said it loud enough for everyone to hear. "I love a good newspaper."

chapter 22

Compromised

Jennifer's mom drove them to the Tremble Zoning Board. Technically, Jennifer had not lied. She explained that they needed to interview Mrs. Boland about beautification.

Her mom was delighted. Being a garden club member plus a PTA leader, she was pro-beautification and in fact, was on the PTA committee making recommendations for beautifying Harris. "Amazing," her mom said, when Jennifer explained why they needed a ride. "The *Slash* is writing some positive news?"

"Come on, Mom," Jennifer said. "We wouldn't do that."

Somehow, Jennifer had forgotten to mention that their interview was about the Bolands' beautification plan to flatten the Willows. Jennifer's philosophy on this could be summed up in seven words: "Why upset Mom for no good reason?"

The coeditors had plenty of time to talk without worrying about Jennifer's mom. She had her headset on and was making calls. It was what Jennifer and Adam loved about cell phones; your parents could be right there supervising you and still had no idea what you were up to.

"Why does Mrs. Boland want to do this in person?" Jennifer asked.

"To scare the crap out of us," said Adam.

"It's working," said Jennifer.

"Never fear," said Adam. He opened his backpack, pulled out a bag of pistachio nuts, and handed her a fistful. "Throw the shells in my backpack when you're done," he said.

"I've never seen you so calm in the face of certain doom," she said. "Usually you're the one falling apart. You do know that we've never been so doomed? If we don't pull this off, we're dead. And if we do, we're dead. Mrs. Boland said herself—she'll shut down the *Slash* or bring in her goons to mind us."

Adam nodded. Jennifer was definitely right. "Want to hear something terrible?" he said. "I'm not sure I care. I am so worn out. Writing the truth about people is too hard. Everyone hates you."

"I don't hate you," said Jennifer, handing him an opened pistachio nut as proof of their enduring friendship.

"You're my coeditor; you have no choice."

He'd already told Jennifer about his disastrous "interview" with Tish. "Me and Tish should be friends," said Adam. "He's a good guy, we both love hoops, but I've pissed him off so bad, he'll never talk to me again. When you're a reporter, you're always keeping your distance from people because you might have to write something bad about them. You're always the outsider."

"Being a reporter doesn't make you an outsider," said Jennifer. "You become a reporter *because* you're an outsider; it suits you."

Adam didn't know if she was right; he just felt a need to get way inside. At that moment, he would have loved being in the middle of a conga line.

He took out his handkerchief, blew his nose,

stared out the window, and shelled some nuts. "Maybe you should've talked to Tish," Adam said. "Maybe me being white made it worse. No matter what I tried, I couldn't get through."

"I doubt I'd be better," said Jennifer. "It probably's a little bit about race stuff, but more rich-poor stuff."

"Please," said Adam. "I'm not rich."

"Compared to Tish we are," Jennifer said. "Look, don't worry so much. Tish might feel different if we pull off this Willows story."

"Right," said Adam. "A happy ending. That would be a miracle."

The van pulled into the circular drive leading to the Tremble offices. "How are you so calm?" Jennifer asked.

"Secret weapon," said Adam.

"Come on, tell me."

"It's better you don't know," he said. "Just don't worry about her cornering us, like in 306. We can leave anytime we want."

"How will I know when it's time?" asked Jennifer.

"When Mrs. Boland starts screaming," he said, "it's time."

"A hint," she pleaded.

"Notice anything about me?" he asked.

"You mean your hair's combed, your shirt's tucked in, and you appear to have bathed within the last month?"

"Right," said Adam. "You said yourself, clean hands and a clean county."

"What's that mean?" asked Jennifer.

"Sorry," he said. "You used up your one hint."

He pulled out his handkerchief and gave a honk.

"Your cold's driving me crazy," she said. "You've had it forever. Are you taking something?"

"Not yet," said Adam. "I still need it."

From the front of the van they could hear Jennifer's mom hanging up. "It's amazing how you can keep on top of everything with these phones," her mom said.

"Really, Mom," said Jennifer. "You are on top of it."

"Amazing," said Adam.

"Now, remember," said Jennifer's mom. "It's an honor having an interview with someone as important as Mrs. Boland. If you make a good impression, someday it could lead to a summer internship at the *Citizen-Gazette* or Boland News 12."

"Right, Mom," said Jennifer. "Working for Boland-vision would be great."

"Amazing," said Adam.

Jennifer's mom was going to the mall and said she'd back in an hour.

"Oh no," said Adam. "We won't need an hour. Twenty minutes, max."

"What?" said Jennifer.

"Trust me," said Adam.

The office was on the top floor of the county building. It was nothing like the shabby, cramped Code Enforcement room in the subbasement where they'd interviewed Herb and Herb the previous fall.

When the attendant opened the elevator gate, Jennifer and Adam stepped onto wall-to-wall carpeting done in a tasteful muted brown. The doors leading to each department were glass, and the desks where the receptionists sat were made of mahogony with large county seals in the middle.

"Hi," Jennifer said. "We're from —"

"They're expecting you," said the receptionist. "Clarence will be out shortly."

Clarence was short, thin, and dressed stylishly in a black three-button suit with a black turtleneck and thick, black-rimmed glasses. He had shaggy hair that was a mix of blond and black, like Mrs. Boland's. Adam had the weirdest thought: Clarence had been dressed by Mrs. Boland.

The coeditors followed Clarence down a hallway and into a magnificent boardroom that was dominated by a glass table so long that a dozen stuffed chairs fit on each side. It was a corner office, and two of the walls were windows that stretched from the floor to the ceiling. Looking out, they could see for miles. Adam thought it would be fun working so high up, like having an office in the climbing tree.

Along the other two walls were several maps. The largest had a banner that read TREMBLE PLANS FOR THE NEXT CENTURY.

Inspirational slogans bordered the maps. One said PERSONAL NEATNESS AND COUNTY BEAUTIFI-CATION GO HAND IN HAND. Another said, EVERYTHING IN ITS PLACE — NOW!! There were two doors, and behind one, Adam guessed, in her private office, lurked Mrs. Boland.

"MRS. BOLAND," Clarence said — and the coeditors snapped to attention — "will be out soon." Clarence walked over to one of the doors and opened it. Adam and Jennifer tensed; they were expecting Mrs. Boland to leap out, like a circus tiger.

"The washroom. Would you mind cleaning your hands?" said Clarence, gesturing to the PERSONAL NEATNESS sign. "It's one of Mrs. Boland's eccentricities."

Adam and Jennifer looked at each other, but said nothing. While Adam was inside, he gave his nose one final blow to freshen up his handkerchief.

Clarence put place mats in front of them so they wouldn't get marks on the glass table. He hurried to the sideboard, where a silver coffeepot along with white, flowered china cups were set up, and poured a spot of coffee into a cup. He tasted it, then hurried to the washroom and returned with the cup, clean and dry.

"You've met Mrs. Boland," said Clarence, "so you know she'll be in a much better mood if everything proceeds in an orderly fashion. Sit up straight. I must say, I'm very pleased. Based on what I heard, I thought you"—he pointed at Adam—"would be problematic. But you look sooo handsome today. Do you play sports? . . . I knew it! And you," he said to Jennifer. "Your outfit is sensational. Is that a Klarey

Konner micromini? . . . I knew it! As they say on Broadway, you've got the figure for it, toots."

Adam was surprised. This Clarence seemed nice.

"Now, I'd be the first to admit," Clarence continued, "Mrs. Boland isn't the easiest person. But she is such a good woman. She really cares about people and making the world better. You probably don't know, but she is the number-one supporter of the Tremble Symphony Orchestra, the Tremble Opera, and the county libraries. It's a lot of work. And sometimes, she just feels she has to do it all herself or it won't be done right. Maybe she's too much that way, but only because she cares. Now she has something to show you. She's very excited. She really hopes you'll like it. We've worked so hard on this. It would mean so much if you could reach a compromise with her. She doesn't want to have to . . . you know . . ."

Adam and Jennifer nodded. Squish them like a bug is what Clarence meant.

Clarence vanished behind door number two, and in seconds Mrs. Boland appeared, also dressed in black. She was carrying three glossy folders. Keeping one, she handed the others to Clarence, who placed them on the mats in front of Adam and Jennifer.

"Read these carefully," said Clarence as he poured Mrs. Boland a cup of coffee.

"Not now, Clarence," Mrs. Boland said in a loud whisper. "It's too soon," and Clarence scooped up the cup and hurried to the washroom again.

Adam felt something he never expected.

That poor lady, he thought. She needs to loosen up.

The coeditors looked over the statement from Mrs. Boland. It was hard for Adam to sit up straight and read at the same time, but the more he went over it, the more impressed he was. The press release had been prepared especially for the *Slash*. It began:

> Just as students at Harris must plan and order their busy days to get all their work done, the great county of Tremble must plan and order where homes are built so all our residents can live peacefully and prosperously side by side. That is precisely the work of the zoning board.

The release went on to say that it was the board's job to give people of all races and backgrounds the opportunity to buy larger and more beautiful homes, and the bigger the homes, the more tax dollars the county receives, and that means more money for Harris Elementary/Middle School.

The release said that through several zoning reforms, Mrs. Boland hoped to encourage construction of million-dollar mini-mansions that would beautify Tremble and wipe out the final pockets of blight.

There was a quote from Mrs. Boland saying, "I must emphasize that every one of these new homes could be purchased by people of all races and backgrounds who work hard and make the sacrifices to afford the Tremble way of life." And then there was a final paragraph about how the county and the Bolands had a long history of cooperation, working together to support the Special Olympics.

When Jennifer finished, she pulled out a notebook. "It's very well written," she said. Clarence was back, and for some reason, this made him beam. "But I have a few things not covered in your response to our questions," Jennifer continued.

"Response to your questions?" said Mrs. Boland, looking at Clarence.

"I think maybe they're confused," said Clarence.

"You are confused," said Mrs. Boland. "This is not a response to your questions. This is your article. This," she said, wiggling the paper at Jennifer, "is what you're going to print. We've written the story for you to make sure it's accurate."

The coeditors looked like a mini-mansion had been dropped on their heads. They did not know what to say.

"But . . . but . . ." Jennifer stammered, "we write our own stories. We'll be glad to include your response. But this isn't the whole story. This doesn't say anything about the boarded-up houses or where families in the Willows will go. They can't afford million-dollar mini-mansions."

"Children," said Mrs. Boland, "I'm not some dictator. I don't tell people where to live. Anyone who has the money can buy a house anywhere in Tremble. The last time we were together, I got very upset. And when I received your questions this week and saw that you were doing ANOTHER WILLOWS STORY!! . . ."

Clarence cleared his throat and Mrs. Boland lowered her voice. "I mean . . . another Willows story, well, my first inclination was . . ."

Adam and Jennifer nodded. Squish them like a bug.

"But Clarence urged compromise," she went on. "As usual, he was right. We worked very hard doing this article for you." She looked at her watch. "Clarence, dear, it's the right time for my coffee."

Mrs. Boland picked up the folder. "This is all your readers need," she said. "Don't make this harder than it has to be. I'm sure they teach you in school that compromise is the essence of democracy. Today, we're going to be like our Founding Fathers at Independence Hall in Philadelphia when they drew up the Constitution. We're not going to leave this room until we've worked out a compromise. I understand you may want to switch a word or two — they always do at the *Citizen-Gazette-Herald-Advertiser* when we give them stories to print. Or maybe you want to break a long paragraph into two shorter ones. I have no problem with that. I'm always willing to compromise. I've cleared my schedule. I will stay until midnight if need be. No one leaves until we're done."

Adam was ready. It was time to go.

He unzipped his backpack and reached for his notebook.

As he yanked it out, pistachio shells flew everywhere, arcing upward, then making distinct *plink*s as they landed on the glass table.

Mrs. Boland and Clarence gasped.

"I am so sorry," said Adam. "What an idiot. Let me clean it up."

Adam grabbed his handkerchief and began wiping the pistachio shells off the table. To Adam, the silence seemed to last forever, though it was just a few seconds. No one except Adam moved.

All eyes were riveted on his handkerchief. Back and forth, back and forth.

Jennifer would later say she was amazed at how clearly Adam's thick streaks of phlegmy snot showed up on that clean glass table.

"FILTH!" bellowed Mrs. Boland, whose face went from pink to purple without pausing at red. "HOW COULD YOU? GET OUT!"

Jennifer was frozen in her seat, but Adam's backpack was zipped and he was on the move. To reach Jennifer quickly, he ran around the near end of the table, behind Clarence and Mrs. Boland. As Adam passed, Mrs. Boland crossed her arms in front of her face, as if Adam was a toxic germ. Rounding the end of the table and heading toward Jennifer, he glimpsed Clarence.

Adam must have been hallucinating.

He could have sworn Clarence winked at him.

Adam grabbed Jennifer's hand and yanked her up. The two ran through the boardroom door, along the hallway, and out the zoning department glass doors. Adam looked frantically side to side. The elevator would take too long. He spotted a red exit sign, and they bolted through that door.

It was the stairs. They raced down six flights, burst into the building lobby, and shot out the front entrance.

Adam looked toward the road, panicked that they were being followed, and as he did, he spotted the prettiest sight ever: Jennifer's blessed mother, turning the Astro van into the driveway.

The coeditors stood panting, trying to catch their breath.

As the van pulled near, Jennifer said, "You can let go of my hand now."

"Oops," Adam said. "Sorry."

"I mean you don't have to . . ."

"I was . . . um . . . you know . . . distracted," said Adam.

"I bet," said Jennifer. "You did that to Mrs. Boland on purpose, didn't you?"

"What?" said Adam.

"That was some secret plan," she said. "You *are* problematic."

They climbed into the van and felt such relief when it moved. For a long time, both were quiet.

"You know," Jennifer finally said. "Mrs. Boland is going to destroy us. We're through."

"I know," said Adam. "But sometimes, when you're doomed, it's nice to go out in style."

chapter 23

The Final Edition

The *Slash* was shut down.

Three days after the paper went home in students' backpacks, the coeditors heard from Mrs. Quigley. She said the Tremble superintendent had talked to some deputy super-duper, who'd ordered the first-assistant-associate-superintendent to call Mrs. Quigley.

"That Bleepin weasel!" said Jennifer. "We know that guy."

"A real kid person," said Adam.

"The very one," said Mrs. Quigley.

What really killed Adam and Jennifer was that they were sure the March/April issue had been their most legendary *Slash* ever, even better than the paper that got Marris fired as principal.

They'd picked Adam's "Science Unfair" story to lead the paper, at the top right of page one, because it affected every Harris student.

And sure enough, the very day the story came out, Mr. Devillio, the world's phoniest science teacher, told their class how happy he was that the fair was going to change.

The Willows story ran top left, a true tale of David versus Goliath: The ordinary Willows people versus the Tremble government and Boland Realty, Inc. Tish might not have talked to them, but Jennifer got interviews with several kids who would have to move away if the Willows became Boland Estates.

The lead was about a family of four. They didn't have enough money to buy their own house in Tremble, the story said, but they rented in the Willows because they wanted their kids to go to a good school like Harris. Jennifer's photo of the family — standing on the sidewalk between their house and a boarded-up house next door — ran under the headline:

WILL THEY DISAPPEAR NEXT?

In the middle of page one was Phoebe's iceberger about the climbing tree being saved, thanks, once again, to the *Slash*.

And across the bottom was the Bully Survey. Mrs. Quigley's bully solution was brilliant as far as the coeditors were concerned. After describing several moving tales of bully victimhood, the article explained the coeditors' concern with the poll's results.

It did *not* list the top ten bullies.

In fact, only one bully vote-getter was named: Adam Canfield. And that's because Adam wrote a first-person sidebar on how crappy he felt about getting even three bully votes and how it made him wonder which three kids hated him.

The story also pointed out that the *Slash* had no intention of censoring the news. So any student who wanted the results just had to make an appointment with the principal. The story said Mrs. Quigley would be delighted to read off the top ten bullies—in alphabetical order—plus the other sixty-five who got at least one vote. And since these students would be displaying such curiosity about bullies, they would be asked to serve on a schoolwide committee to reduce bullying.

/////

"Guess how many kids came to see me about the bully results?" said Mrs. Quigley. "Four!"

"That's all?" said Jennifer.

"Kids are smarter than adults," said Mrs. Quigley. "They know how sleepy you get sitting on committees."

"Your plan was great," said Adam. But he didn't feel great. "You think there's any way we can trick Bleepin into keeping the *Slash* going?"

"Adam," said Mrs. Quigley, "you know Bleepin wasn't the real culprit; he was just the trained seal they sent to do the trick. You know who's responsible."

Mrs. Quigley told them that a few days before the *Slash* came out, she received a very "heated" call from a Boland assistant, warning if the "correct" story wasn't printed, the next call would be the end of the *Slash*.

"That's outrageous," said Jennifer. "You should've seen their 'correct' story."

"I did," said Mrs. Quigley. "They e-mailed it."

"You didn't tell us?" said Jennifer.

"I liked yours better."

"Mrs. Quigley," said Jennifer, "you stood up to the Bolands?"

"Believe me, it was no big deal," she said. "I'm only the acting principal. I'm leaving in June. What could they do, kick me out two months early?"

"You did that for us?" said Jennifer.

"Oh no," said Mrs. Quigley, "I did it because I believe truth must win out. And sometimes the poor, abused truth needs help."

Adam was amazed. He never knew it. A brave principal was a school newspaper's best friend.

"While we're on a roll," said Mrs. Quigley, "more bad news." The Boland Foundation and *Citizen-Gazette-Herald-Advertiser* had just announced the winners of their student newspaper awards, and the *Slash* was the only paper in all Tremble that did not win a citation of excellence.

"What a joke," said Adam. "The *Slash* is the best student paper anywhere; it's way better than that ridiculous *Citizen-Gazette-Herald-Poopetizer.*"

"These literary awards," said Mrs. Quigley, "can get a little political sometimes."

/////

311

Adam and Jennifer were numb. They were exhausted, and though they didn't tell anyone, there was a part of them that felt enormous relief at not having to worry about the next issue of the *Slash*. But it was not sweet relief; it was guilt-ridden relief.

When Adam bumped into *Slash* staff members — reporters, editors, photographers, typists, fact-checkers — they talked about how outraged they were and vowed to fight to their deaths to save the *Slash*.

Adam, on the other hand, could not feel a thing. He had been outraged by the Bolands, outraged by the science unfair, outraged by the bully vote, out-raged by the threat to the climbing tree.

Now it appeared that Adam's brain was suffering an outrage outage.

If he saw *Slash* staffers in the halls, he walked the other way.

The staff talked endlessly about what they planned to do, but without their coeditors, they were lost. Everyone had a different plan.

Phoebe wanted to picket Mrs. Boland for the rest of her stinking life, no matter where she went, showing up at every public meeting and sneezing in her face.

Sammy favored a consumer boycott of Boland-vision Cable, with families stopping their cable service.

A typist suggested getting the key to 306 from Eddie the janitor, having staff members lock themselves in the newsroom, and then going on a hunger strike, refusing to take even sweetened fruit juices.

Shadow was sure Mr. Johnny Stack could save them.

Phoebe collected all these ideas into a Take Action Now! list that she e-mailed to Jennifer, who showed it to Adam. Their suggestions touched the coeditors, but privately, Jennifer told Adam that she wouldn't give a penny for their thoughts.

Picketing, hunger strikes, and boycotts only worked if the media gave you coverage, and no one in the local press cared about the *Slash*. This had broken the coeditors' weary hearts: No one picked up their great Willows story. Not Bolandvision 12 or the *Citizen-Gazette,* of course, but not the local radio stations either or the online news services — not one blog.

As for Sammy's idea to boycott Boland cable — Tremble citizens might complain about cable costing a fortune and being a monopoly, but as far as Adam could tell, they considered cable a basic necessity, like air and water.

Nor did Jennifer believe that Mr. Johnny Stack

could solve this one. He had clearly given Shadow a lifetime's worth of good advice, but Jennifer didn't see how ignoring the fools would fix this problem.

It took a few weeks. He barely noticed at first. Then slowly, very slowly, something began to stir inside Adam. It wasn't in his brain. Closer to his chest. Not that old outrage exactly. More a longing. He began having a vague sense that something—it almost felt like a good friend—was absent from his life. There was a void. A hole.

Then, one morning he woke up missing Phoebe.

That terrified him, and he went looking for Jennifer.

They had to do something to save the *Slash*!

As usual, she was way ahead of him. She'd been spending hours on her computer, researching. She compiled a list of organizations that seemed like they might care if a newspaper were shut down or if people were forced to leave their homes: the American Civil Liberties Union; the National Coalition Against Censorship; Investigative Reporters and Editors Inc.; the NAACP; the United States Department of Housing and Urban Development's fair housing division.

And she wrote to them all.

Adam had his own plan, which was way simpler. He called Erik Forrest, the globe-trotting war correspondent and Mr. Mom memoirist.

Forrest had once said if Adam ever needed help, just call.

"Hey, Mr. Forrest, it's Adam Canfield of the *Slash*. Remember me? From the bookstore in Tremble . . ."

"Remember you?" said Mr. Forrest. "I have your story taped on my terminal."

"Really?" said Adam. "Great."

"Oh yeah," said Mr. Forrest. "How could I forget you? In the entire twelve-city tour, I did interviews with everyone from *People* magazine to the Jason's Daddy Stays at Home blog, and to the best of my knowledge, you were the only one to call the book *stupid*. I had no idea you were such a master of literary criticism. Others called it 'light' or 'breezy,' but you obviously don't mince words. 'Stupid.' Yes, I remember 'stupid.'"

"Geez, Mr. Forrest," said Adam, "that wasn't the real point. I think you're great. What I was trying to say . . ."

"Be quiet, Adam, I got the point. Why do you think I have your story taped on my terminal? I'll tell you, that book tour cured me of ever again writing for easy money. Now, I do believe I would have come to that realization on my own, but meeting you—it was the turning point. That little sidebar you did on Erik Forrest's four tips to great reporting—I realized I'd stopped following my own advice."

"Wow, Mr. Forrest," said Adam. "Something I wrote helped a famous writer like you?"

"Yup. I'm like an alcoholic in recovery. I have not been on a cable news show for thirty-seven straight days."

"Boy," said Adam, "this makes me feel like doing a little follow-up story."

"If you don't mind, Adam," said Mr. Forrest, "I'd like to keep this conversation private. Just two reporters talking shop. That OK?"

"Oh sure, Mr. Forrest, no problem. Anyway, that's not why I called."

Adam reminded Forrest of the Willows story, and then told him all the latest details, including Adam's messy handkerchief trick and Mrs. Boland's shutting down the *Slash.*

As bad as the news was, it was exciting to tell. Mr. Forrest really appreciated the juicy reporting details, like finding Harris kids who'd have to leave the Willows and getting Reverend Shorty to talk on the record.

"What a gotcha," he said.

Adam mentioned all the groups that Jennifer had been sending letters to and Mr. Forrest said that was good. But if any of these groups went to court to fight the shutdown of the *Slash,* Mr. Forrest said, it could take years for a final decision.

He said he knew a simpler, faster alternative. "I know someone who'd love to do that Willows story."

"Who?" asked Adam.

"Don't worry about that," said Mr. Forrest. "Just e-mail me a copy of the story and Reverend Shorty's phone number."

Adam kept thanking him. "You think this story will be out by next week?" Adam asked.

"Oh no," said Mr. Forrest. "Even though the

Slash did it, the reporter will still have to go to the Willows and do all the stuff you guys did— interview the families and the minister, check out the boarded-up houses, get a comment from the Bolands. That takes time."

chapter 24

The Uncruelest Month

Adam once had overheard Marsha Tiffany Glickman, editor of *Sketches,* the Harris literary magazine, say it is a well-known poetic fact that April is the cruelest month. But that year, in the Tri-River Region, April was the warmest and sweetest Adam had ever seen. Spring was full upon them, and for days, Adam woke to bright sunshine and a balmy southerly breeze off the river. Big white clouds drifted by, lit up by the sun, and more than once, Adam thought how nice it would be to climb up on one and float away.

It was a quieter time for the coeditors, though they were quiet-busy. Busy with their spring sports—Adam with baseball, Jennifer with tennis. Busy preparing for the spring concert—Adam had a jazz band concert, Jennifer a string recital. Busy readying music solos for the state competition; busy drilling at before-school/after-school classes for the state tests; busy prepping for the Quiz Bowl Gladiator regionals; busy with the Math Olympiad quarterfinals; busy with the Geography Challenge Countdown to Total Dominance.

For these activities, their parents, their teachers, and their coaches told them where to stand, when to start, and when to go home.

The *Slash* had been different: Adam and Jennifer had to think their own thoughts.

There were, of course, still things to worry about. The court date in the snow-shoveling case was fast approaching, and Adam hadn't written what he would tell the judge. A pink paper arrived, a subpoena, requiring him to appear in connection with Indictment No. SCI962 N-09, People of the County of Tremble versus Timothy Cox. There was a lengthy Victim's Statement form and Victim's Restitution form full of boxes to be checked. Adam was supposed to give his recommendation, ranging from a felony charge carrying four years in prison down to voluntary counseling. He sat at the computer, but each time, he got stalled and instant-messaged friends about stupid stuff.

Adam and Jennifer knew nobody missed the *Slash* more than Phoebe. She wasn't quite as over-programmed as they were. She missed front-page glory. She missed talking with actual middle-school kids. She missed Jennifer, the world's nicest coeditor. She even admitted to Adam that she missed him. "There were some days you weren't that crabby," she said.

Phoebe feared she'd never be famous again.

Recycling Club was fun, she told Jennifer, and being third-grade recycling captain was a huge honor. But winning a certificate for best recycling idea of the month — on recycled paper, of course — was not the same as front-page glory. Big kids didn't give her high fives in the hallways because she won a recycling certificate.

The coeditors had discovered that a few days a week after school, Phoebe still sneaked up to 306 to see, if by any chance, the door was open. Each time, she'd say, "Come on, baby," and hold her breath five seconds for good luck, then turn the knob, feeling full of confidence.

It was always locked.

Sometimes, Phoebe leaned against the door on tiptoe, shielding her eyes and peering through the window. Just looking into 306 gave her a warm feeling. Everything had been left as it was — the posters, the iced-tea cans and chocolate-milk cartons. Phoebe could see old newspapers, drafts of stories, and photos scattered on desks. She could see her favorite couch for reporting icebergers.

She'd stare at the picnic-bench conference table, where she had argued about the climbing tree story with two middle-school coeditors. That's why she loved the *Slash*, she told Jennifer — ideas were more important here than what grade a person was in.

Was it really over?

Some days, she stood at the door on tiptoe so long, her legs got wobbly. Once, as she shifted her weight to steady herself, she bumped into someone and gasped.

Turning, she was surprised to see Shadow.

"What are you doing here?" Phoebe asked.

"I don't know," said Shadow. "What are you doing here?"

"I was—uh—making sure the door was locked," said Phoebe. "So no one steals anything from the newsroom."

"Me, too," said Shadow.

"OK, then," said Phoebe.

"OK, then," said Shadow, and they hurried down the hallway in opposite directions.

"What are you doing here?" Adam whispered.

Shadow was sitting on the other side of the wooden gate, in the spectators' section of the courtroom. He looked positively giddy, waving a pink subpoena at Adam. Adam turned and stared toward the front again. He propped his head up with his hands to steady himself; inside, he felt like Jell-O.

He sat at a table in the front of the courtroom, alongside the two prosecutors, whose job it was to put bad guys in jail.

At the other table, across the aisle, sat the defense attorney, whose job it was to keep people out of jail. Next to the defense attorney was the kid who had punched Adam, Timmy Cox, Shadow's older brother. He was dressed in an orange jumpsuit worn by jail inmates. Two tall court officers with white shirts, silver badges, and guns guarded him.

"ALL RISE!" a court clerk called out. "The Honorable Judge Carol Stokinger presiding." A woman in a black robe entered from a rear door and sat at the bench.

The judge's voice sounded nicer than Adam had expected. As she described the case, Adam glanced around. Sitting behind him in the spectator area was a whole rooting section for Adam. It included his parents, several of his parents' friends, Danny, his grandma, an aunt and uncle, Jennifer's mom, and Jennifer. Shadow was there with a woman — most likely his tenth or eleventh caseworker. Probably the judge wanted Shadow to talk about his brother, too.

Adam was thinking how weird it was that all kinds of crazy stuff happened in the real world like people shooting each other and blowing up each other and then the same people came into a courtroom, sat close together, and said, "thank you" and "excuse me," like life was civilized.

The judge explained that the other four teenagers had pleaded guilty, as had this young man, Timmy

Cox. But because he appeared to be the ringleader and faced a stiffer sentence, the judge said she wanted to hear from the affected party before deciding on a fair punishment.

There was more talk that Adam didn't listen to, and then, before he knew it, the judge asked him to speak.

Adam stood and held the statement he'd written. He began reading, but the necktie his mom made him wear must have cut off the oxygen to his brain, because the words on the paper were blurry. So he stopped, put down the paper, and just talked.

He said he hadn't actually been too hurt by the robbery—hardly at all really—that it had passed in a blur and the worst part was afterward, when it was on TV and everyone at school knew, and every time he did something a little stupid, his parents were scared he was cracking up, when he was actually just doing something a little stupid.

He told the judge about the bully survey the *Slash* had done and how they'd realized they'd made a mistake to single out the top ten bullies, but how he thought this shoveling case was different—it was more serious—and not just because it was Adam.

These kids had broken the law, Adam said, for no good reason, pointing out they could have gotten a ton of shoveling jobs and made lots of money.

Then Adam talked about how he'd become friends with Shadow and how he knew from Shadow that this older brother had given him fourteen stitches on the head and that, in Adam's opinion, this made the whole case even less forgivable.

The next thing Adam said surprised him, not having had a clue he was going to say it until the words came out. Adam told the judge how much his parents loved him, how they did everything in their power to get him to turn out half-decent and how, without them, he'd probably be some pathetic person in the dirt. And he said that he knew Shadow and his brother lived without their parents and how much a kid would want to get adopted by nice grown-ups and how having a brother like Shadow, if you were trying to get yourself adopted and put on a good show for strangers, might make you embarrassed and angry.

"I don't know which is the right box to check," Adam said, "but I think probably he deserves to be punished pretty good. But I also think maybe if there was some way he and Shadow could get to be real

brothers again, like some expert could show them —
that would be great. I can't imagine what it's like
growing up without family. My family saves me
practically every second. Family and a few friends —
that's everything. I will admit, Shadow can drive
you a little crazy sometimes, but he's a great guy.
He's an unbelievable worker — you should see him
sweep the puddles at the Rec courts. And I think
he's more proud of his Roger Clemens rookie card
than Roger Clemens's own mother. And he's really
important for our school paper. He's like the best
fact-checker we got. The last issue of the *Slash* — he
caught a dozen mistakes that the so-called normal
kids missed."

"To be exact, it was thirteen mistakes," said a
voice from the spectator section. "Six spelling mistakes, three wrong addresses, two math mistakes, and
two missing words. Six plus three plus two plus two
is definitely not twelve or a dozen, same thing. Six
plus three plus two plus two is definitely thirteen."

Outside the courtroom, in the black-and-white
marble lobby, the grown-ups took turns hugging
Adam and telling him how proud they were. To go

327

with her hug, Jennifer gave him a little kiss on the cheek and whispered something in his ear. Shadow gave Adam one of his life-skills handshakes.

"It's your day, kid," said Danny, handing Adam a copy of the *New York Times* national edition he'd picked up at the courthouse newsstand.

Adam looked at the headlines but didn't know what Danny was talking about.

"Flip it over," said Danny. There on the bottom left of the front page, below the fold, was their story. The headline read "Rich Family Gobbles Up Suburb's Last Affordable Housing."

The byline was Erik Forrest.

Adam skimmed it, his eyes popping out when he saw the word *Slash*. In the last graph before the story jumped to page sixteen was a sentence saying "Details of the Bolands' efforts to buy up the Willows were first reported last month in the *Slash*, the student newspaper of Harris Elementary/Middle School."

"Geez," said Adam. "That's us. This might help, huh?"

"Could," said Danny.

Jennifer wanted to go right back to Harris to show Mrs. Quigley, get a meeting with that Bleepin idiot, and make a plan to save the *Slash*.

Not Adam. "Hey, Danny," Adam said. "You feeling well enough to go for a skip?"

"You know," said Danny, "I think I am."

"OK to invite a few friends?" Adam asked.

"That would be fine," said Danny, watching as the three raced out the courthouse revolving door, down the granite steps, and across the sidewalk. They were careful not to step on any lines or cracks — Jennifer had called it. As they reached the parking lot, Shadow was in the lead, Jennifer a close second, and Adam was lagging behind. But he didn't care. The sky had never looked bluer or the grass greener, and besides, he was the only one who knew which car was Danny's.